KEEP COOL,
MR. JONES

KEEP COOL, MR. JONES

Timothy Fuller

PERENNIAL LIBRARY

Harper & Row, Publishers, New York
Cambridge, Philadelphia, San Francisco, Washington
London, Mexico City, São Paulo, Singapore, Sydney

Published by arrangement with Little, Brown & Company
in association with the Atlantic Monthly Press.

First PERENNIAL LIBRARY edition published 1987.

LIBRARY OF CONGRESS CATALOG CARD NUMBER: 86-46064
ISBN: 0-06-080866-7
87 88 89 90 91 OPM 10 9 8 7 6 5 4 3 2 1

KEEP COOL,
MR. JONES

1

"This way!" Dot Dexter hissed and yanked his arm.

"I'm sorry. I ..." And then the sweaty paw of the Unitarian minister's wife was in his hand and he was off again in the other direction.

My God, Jones thought, will it never end? How could I have allowed myself...

"Other way, son!" This was from the minister himself, accompanied by a solid shove.

"I'm terribly sorry. I have never..."

"Here!" It was Dot again, grabbing his arm and swinging him around.

He stopped apologizing for his ineptness and simply allowed the others, who were after all accomplished square dancers, to shove, prod, and jerk him through the nightmarish figure. They did it with fixed, polite smiles which he refused to return.

He had, he realized, been betrayed into this frightful exhibition by alcohol and a pretty face. For nearly two hours he had held out and then

Dot Dexter had dragged him from the bar with sly taunts and much provocative batting of her big brown eyes. "You're being so very, very superior, Jupiter," she had said, standing close to him. "It maddens me!"

That, of course, had done it. She knew how he disliked this dogged use of his unfortunate schoolboy nickname but beyond this she was perceptive enough to understand how he had actually been feeling. "I didn't think it showed," he had answered, but he had gone out with her nevertheless onto the floor.

This was Jack Maney's second annual barn dance to swell the Saxon Public Library's book purchasing fund and Jupiter had dressed himself grotesquely in a pink shirt and dungarees and agreed to attend only because his wife, Betty, had, in one bleak period of her premarital life, learned to square dance and unaccountably still considered it fun. In a white peekaboo blouse and black ballet skirt she was twirling now, in another set across the barn floor, with graceful abandon.

It would never end! Fat, red-faced Howie Howland, the caller, must have spotted him out here and decided to make him suffer. What had he ever done to Howland? Three years ago Howland, a real estate agent, had sold them their large, rather ugly, colonial house here in Saxon but...

"To the left!" Dot ordered and pushed him so that his head snapped. "There!"

2

He had a good mind to tell this woman what he really thought of her flashy, facile water colors! There was perspiration now on her nose and cheeks and her thick, gray-streaked black bangs bounced without allure. He must get over, and soon, this lingering adolescent weakness for dark-eyed women. She was forty and foolish and there were even rumors that she had shoddy little affairs. Poor Harry! Dexter, her husband, had left an advertising job in New York to buy a blacksmith shop here in town where he made replicas of old hinges and latches as well as weather vanes and individualized signs for front lawns. He was pleasant enough although he often spoke fervently, while puffing his pipe, about how fine it was to get back to the simpler things in life. Such as square dancing.

As to Jones, the death and will of an eccentric but happily well-heeled uncle shortly after the war had allowed him, at thirty-five, to quit his job as an assistant professor of Fine Arts at Harvard. He and Betty had chosen to live in the country out of a vague but so far accurate belief that it was a good place to raise their three children and he was now engaged in unhurriedly writing a lengthy volume concerned with the relationship between painting and politics down through the years. They had chosen Saxon—a town of fifteen hundred people, part rural, part suburban, lying well out on the wheel of Boston's dwindling universe—simply because a house had been available there at not too staggering a price. Saxon was a rather aggressively community-minded town made up of stanch Republicans and a small, vocal group of transplanted urban liberals, like the Dexters, but three years as an officer in the Navy had conditioned him to keep his peace at appropriate moments and he got along well enough with his neighbors.

At last, as all things must, the dance ended.

"Now was that so bad?" They all looked at him happily.

He felt emotionally unequipped to answer this question and merely bowed to the group and rubbed his leg. "Old Ping-pong injury," he panted. "Acts up from time to time. You'll excuse me?"

He limped away to the bar, pursued relentlessly by Dot. "You could get it. It just takes practice. It's really fun when you know how!"

"I refuse to believe it. To me it has all the charm of an evening of mixed basketball. Find yourself another partner before that hideous music begins again."

"You're a meany!" She wrinkled her nose at him uselessly.

At the rear of the barn, which had been remodeled into a huge summer playroom, was a small permanent bar presided over now by a bright, broken-nosed youth named Joe Bateman who had been doing a desultory business, among these dance-mad fanatics, at fifty cents a drink. The liquor itself had been donated to the cause by their host, Jack Maney, who operated a chain of prosperous wayside taverns.

"I saw you out there, Jonesy," Bateman said, "but I had the courtesy to avert my eyes."

"Thanks, Joe."

"You'll be needing something now. A wee, you'll pardon the expression, doch-an-dorris?"

"By all means."

"And the lady?"

Dot shook her head. "Not now. Have you seen Harry, Joe?"

Joe had not seen Harry, and Dot, convinced at last that Jupiter was through dancing for the night, hurried off in search of another partner.

"I'll tell you a secret, Jonesy," Joe said, handing across his highball. "The world is mad. *Mad, do you hear?*"

He grabbed his hair, grinned, and poured himself a drink. Joe, who had worked for a time as a bartender in one of Maney's taverns, was ostensibly employed as the farm foreman but was more accurately a fishing, hunting, and drinking companion for his boss. To Saxon, the Maney menage was a vaguely sinister, vaguely humorous curiosity. Although the taverns bore such stylish names as THE DRUM AND FIFE, THE BLUE GOOSE, and THE PEWTER TANKARD and were well known to parched and respectable motorists by their long low roofs, red paint, and huge fieldstone chimneys, Maney remained, in local opinion, a saloonkeeper with overtones of the dark days of gangsters and bootleggers. On the farm itself, as a handy way to take a tax loss, Maney raised pheasants, the birds with wings clipped being turned before slaughter into a wired ten-acre field planted to cultivated blueberries. This was held by most Saxons to be an outrageously extravagant procedure but the result, as Jupiter knew, was a tasty bird indeed. Each year's crop was frozen and distributed as gifts to influential friends throughout the state. To the Boston papers, in which he appeared infrequently as a sports follower and guest at Democratic Party functions, Maney was known as "the jovial and popular restaurateur." He gave large rambling parties to which Betty and Jupiter, for no very good reason, were invariably invited. They had tried several times to return his hospitality but it happened that on each occasion Maney had been "out of town." He seemed quite content, as was Jupiter, to keep their relationship on an impersonal basis. It was barely possible, too, that Maney was socially ashamed of his wife, a shockingly beautiful blonde from Texas who had complicated her speech pattern by three years in the line at various Broadway night spots. Known to everyone as "Slim," she was, to Jupiter, the finest sight for miles around. He looked around now for a glimpse of her. The dancing had started again but he couldn't see her on the floor.

"Where's Slim?" he asked Bateman.

"Haven't seen her for some time," Joe said.

"For that matter I haven't seen the boss for some time. But it's not up to me to look after them. Yes, Mrs. Wren?"

They had been joined by a thin, sixtyish lady who said, "Oh, nothing. Nothing for me. I was looking for the doctor. I wondered if either of you had seen him?"

"Not lately, ma'am."

Dr. Wren, a retired dentist, owned the oldest Cape Cod house in town which he had named, perhaps inevitably, The Wrens' Nest. Both the Wrens were bird watchers, herb growers, and stout champions of such wild growing edibles as milkweed, nettles, fiddle fronds, and skunk cabbage. Crouching among her hanging copper pots Mrs. Wren, Jupiter knew, baked her own bread in her original Dutch oven from water-ground meal procured by mail from a restored mill in Connecticut.

"I haven't seen him for over half an hour and I'm a little worried," she said.

She had good reason to be worried. Although Wren would on a cold day ceremoniously offer a visitor a hot buttered rum made from an ancient recipe, Jupiter had discovered by the accident of running out of gas in front of the Nest one evening that the doctor was a secret and prodigious drinker of the cheapest kind of whiskey which he laid up in case lots. That particular evening he had drunkenly demonstrated how he pitched his empties down an abandoned well in his back yard, thus removing them from the revealing contents of his trash pile. By speaking very little to anyone after four o'clock in the afternoon he had apparently concealed his unhappy habit from the town, and Jupiter, although the Wrens had not asked him to, had respected their secret.

"I'll see if I can find him," he said.

"I thought he might be in the car but I've looked there and..."

"I'll find him."

He left the bar and threaded his way gingerly through the frenzied dancers to the wide barn door. There were perhaps a hundred and fifty at the party and, except for a row of elderly spectators along one wall, they all seemed to be out on the floor, natives and newcomers alike. He noticed that his place had been taken by Phil Gaudy, a selectman and house painter, who was swinging Dot with determined assurance. It was all very democratic and, though he could be wrong, just the slightest bit phony.

Outside and in welcome relief from the strident three-piece band he listened for a moment to the peepers peeping in a nearby swamp. A full May moon beamed down upon him and he lit a cigarette. Where could Wren have got to? There were no lights on in the barn's basement where, he knew, there were rooms for incubating, brooding, and killing the pheasants and a spacious walk-in deep freeze for holding the finished product. Away from the barn was a stable, newly built and topped by one of Harry

Dexter's more ambitious weather vanes, featuring a setter dog and two rising pheasants. There was a light showing there and he wandered over. Inside was Slim Maney talking to her handsome Palomino stallion.

"Oh, hi, honey," she said and raised a dark highball to him in greeting. She was tall and tanned and wore her pale blond hair long and loose on her shoulders in much the manner of the stallion. She had on a pair of revealingly tailored, cream-colored frontier pants, gold sandals, and a brown silk shirt piped western style in yellow. In that pose and costume, against the horse's head and the fluorescent lit, pine-paneled stall, she looked precisely like a beer advertisement depicting Gracious Country Living. "What a stinkin' party, huh, Jonesy?"

"Oh, come now, Slim."

"Honest. What's with this square dancing, honey? It does nothin' for me, nothin' at all."

"I'm surprised at you. Don't you know it's authentic folk art?"

"Art, shmart." She curled her upper lip, destroying for an instant her normal effect of almost ethereal beauty. He shook his head, marveling at her.

Maney's two English setters were leaping against their chain-link barrier at the end of the stable and Jupiter walked down and scratched their ears through the wire. "You just don't like people, Slim."

"You! I do so like people! I love people!"

"You're moody."

She examined this thought for a moment, tapping the edge of the glass against her teeth. "Uh, huh. I s'pose I am. But you know what kind of a party I go for, Jonesy? I like a bunch of screwballs all together in a big old room and you have a stack of records on the machine turned up loud. Everybody's all likkered up and yellin' and then there'll be this old smoochy record come on and people will dance. Together, I mean. None of this swing your partners, loopy-do. Nyaah!" She took a firm pull at her drink to emphasize the point.

"I'm very fond of you, Slim," he said and regretfully turned away from the setters. "Have you seen Dr. Wren wandering around anywhere?"

"No. I've been looking for Jack myself. I just bet a dollar he's ducked out. I just bet. Except Joe is still around. If Joe was gone too, I'd be sure. Those two." She paused, apparently to see if he had any comment to make and when he didn't she shrugged. "You're a screwball, too, Jonesy."

"Why, Slim?"

"Just you are. Take now. We're out here and you're married and you don't make a pass at me."

"I'll admit that's strange."

"Sure. If you were single it'd be because of Jack but you're *married.*"

"I'm an old-fashioned gentleman."

"Gentleman, shmentleman." She looked at the door and waved. "Hello, Tommy, honey. Come in."

"Hello, Slim, Jupe."

Tom Madison, slight, young, bespectacled, and shy, stood uncertainly at the door of the stable. He was the editor and publisher of a small monthly magazine called the *Moderator*, devoted principally to the attractions of rural New England living. It featured articles on antiques, famous shipwrecks, clambakes, and the like, ran photographs of covered bridges, lobster boats, and elm-shaded church yards, and had yet to lose less than ten thousand dollars a year. "I was looking for Mother. They want to make the drawing on the television set and she's supposed to be in charge."

"I just know I'm going to win it," Slim said. "I know. And we have three already. We have one in our bedroom, of all the damned places."

"She was with Jack the last time I saw her," Tom said. "But that was almost an hour ago."

"I haven't seen Jack for that long," said Slim.

"Do you think they could have gone down to the house?" Tom asked.

"I was just there, honey. Oh, I know where they are, sure 'nough."

"Where?"

"They're rattin'."

"Rattin'?" Jupiter demanded.

"Shootin' rats at the town dump, of course.

Only, I don't know. Do you think your mother would be doin' that, honey?"

The vision of his mother rat hunting at the dump with Jack Maney was a strong one for Tom but he struggled with it manfully. "I don't really think so." He winked at Jupiter. "Not at night, anyway. I mean with the party and all."

"And the television set," Jupiter said.

"Well, maybe no," Slim allowed.

"I really can't think where the heck she could have got to." Tom waved vaguely and left.

"Now you see if Joe wasn't in the barn making drinks I'd know they were rattin'. They've been doin' it every night for a week. They take a big old light and a rifle and sit there on the truck with a bottle between them. I went once but they won't let me go anymore."

"Why?"

"I shot Jack that one time."

"Couple of meanies," said Jupiter, fascinated.

"Oh, it was really shameful what I did, honey. I shot him right in the leg and we had to go to the doctor."

She looked straight at him out of her large blue eyes and it wasn't in his heart to accuse her of guile. "Now, listen for a minute, Slim. Jack's missing. Mrs. Madison is missing. Dr. Wren is missing. And from what Dot said, a while ago, Harry Dexter may be missing, too. Where could they be? What could they be up to?"

"That sweet man, he sends me so."

"Who?" he asked wearily.

"Harry, love him. Do you know what that man did for me?"

"No."

"He learned to shoe horses."

"Well, he's a blacksmith. That's his trade."

"Honest, Jonesy, he never knew how to shoe horses. We used to have to take Stardust way over to a real blacksmith in the trailer. But Harry studied up and now he does it for us, doesn't he, sweetie?" She kissed the Palomino, leaving a slight smear of lipstick just above its nose. "But they wouldn't still be in there."

"In where?"

"Jack and Mrs. Madison and Dr. Wren and Harry," she said. "They went to look at the pheasants, the dead ones in the freezer. But, goodness, that was a long time ago and it's so cold in that room, they wouldn't have stayed in there five minutes. Not five minutes, Jonesy."

Jupiter felt a brief tremor go up and down his spine. "You're sure they were together, when they went to look at the pheasants?"

"It was Tom saying he'd seen his mother with Jack brings it back. They were talking about the pheasants and then they started off down there. But they couldn't be there, honey. Not still, it's too cold. And anyway the lights are out down there and Jack is always awfully careful about lights and locking the door. Joe made him put a padlock on the freezer because last year at the dance someone stole some of them. Imagine

13

anyone stealing pheasants! What some people will do!"

"Maybe we ought to have a look at that freezer, Slim."

"You don't, sure 'nough, think they've been in there all this time?"

"I sure 'nough don't know. But they've got to be somewhere. Let's go."

They walked quickly down to the barn and around to the basement door. She found the light switch and snapped it on, revealing a small spotless room with a stainless sink, counters, and several doors, including the one to the freezer room. This door, Jupiter saw at once, was firmly padlocked.

"Now there, you see," she said. Upstairs they could hear the music and the shuffle of the dancers' feet. She put one hand over her head and spun in a circle. "You'd think they'd get plum tired out."

He went to the freezer door, shrugged, flipped the padlock with his finger, and noticed the light switch by the door read ON. His spinal tremor returned more vigorously. He turned the switch off and on a few times, put his head against the door, and almost at once heard a dull thumping from inside. He thumped back with what he hoped was reassurance and turned to Slim, who was watching him with one hand over her mouth. "Who's got a key to this thing?"

14

"Jack's like to be tearing mad! I swear I don't see how..."

"Has Joe got a key?" he demanded, and when she nodded: "Go get it, Slim. Hurry up. Beat it."

When he pushed her she loped away toward the stairs and was back almost at once followed by Joe Bateman, who was wiping his hands on his bar apron and muttering.

"This is all we needed tonight," he said, getting out his keys. "This is a pretty kettle, you might say, of fish."

Jupiter moved away and Joe unsnapped the lock and swung the heavy door open into the room. Maney, in shirt sleeves, stepped out and to one side and Mrs. Madison, with Maney's plaid dinner jacket pulled tight around her shoulders, followed him. Behind her was Harry Dexter and then, staggering a little so that Maney had to catch his arm, came Dr. Wren. They were all out of breath and trembling from the cold.

"About time, kid," Maney said to Joe. He was a big man going a little fat and gray and he began to blow on his fingers, his shoulders hunched up around his ears. "What happened?"

Joe looked at Slim and she looked at Jupiter and then they were all looking at him. Jupiter coughed. "I don't wish to cause you any alarm, friends, but maybe you've been murdered."

2

If the town of Saxon could be said to have a Grande Dame—and there were a number of residents ready to say it—then Mrs. J. Parker Madison was it. She had all the wealth, background, and steely self-assertion required for the job. It was said she had caused the removal of two ministers, a high school principal, and the entire slate of the Saxon Community Association in one wrathful eighteen-month period. She lived with her son, Tom, in a large house on the square, took long, tweedy walks in the roughest weather, and had undoubtedly contributed her bit to the heart attack that had finally carried off J. Parker who, during his lifetime, had doubled a sizable fortune in wool.

"In that case," she now said, out of the silence that had greeted Jupiter's startling announcement, "I think we should inform the police."

"That shouldn't be difficult," said Jupiter. "Chief Howland is upstairs calling the dances."

"Oh, yes," said Mrs. Madison, her enthusiasm

for the police dwindling a trifle. "Chief How-land."

Jack Maney, limping slightly from the rifle wound in his leg, went to the sink and turned on the tap. "Put your hands under here, Mrs. Madison. Let 'em thaw out gradually. What we need is a shot, Joe. Fetch a jug, lad."

"Oh, Jack, honey, you'd like to freeze in there!" said Slim and embraced him.

"What happened?" Maney asked and when Jupiter had explained about the padlock he said quietly, "Strike me dead." He didn't seem greatly upset by it all.

Bateman returned with a bottle and Maney said, "Thanks, Joe. Here, Mrs. Madison, have a charge."

"Oh, no. Really!"

"Oh, come on, dear, take it," Slim urged. "It's what you need. For chills."

Surprisingly Mrs. Madison timidly took the bottle and raised it gingerly to her lips. It was at this moment that Tom Madison appeared at the outside door and, seeing his mother thus employed, exclaimed, "Why, Mother! So this is where you've been all this time!"

Mrs. Madison choked and while Slim beat her vigorously on the back Jupiter explained the situation to Tom. Harry Dexter had sat down and removed his shoes, and was silently rubbing his toes. Dr. Wren maneuvered himself into possession of the whiskey and they all listened fascinated to the clicking of the bottle's neck against the dentist's chattering false teeth. Finished, Wren stretched out flat on the floor.

"Feeling faint, Doc?" Joe asked, bending over him.

"He's pooped out from jumping up and down in there. We all are," Maney said. "We were beginning to get low on oxygen. It was that as much as the cold."

Jupiter knelt down and loosened Wren's collar. There appeared to be enough color in his face and he was breathing more easily. He was a tall angular man with a small white mustache and gold-rimmed glasses which were now steamed over, making it impossible to tell if his eyes were open. Jupiter removed the glasses and Wren said, opening his eyes, "You sure... murder?"

"I really think so," said Jupiter. "It would be a poor practical joke and I don't see how anyone could have locked it by accident."

Wren closed his eyes and sighed.

"Tom, dear," Mrs. Madison said, "run upstairs and ask Chief Howland to come down."

"Whoa! Hold up, lad," said Maney. "Let's not go off..."

"Half-cocked," Joe broke in, quickly.

"Check." Maney smiled at Bateman. "This thing will bear some..." He paused, waiting for Joe.

"Looking into?" Joe suggested. "Investigation?"

18

"Either one," said Maney. Jupiter had heard them play this game before.

"Now, you boys, don't start that old thing again," Slim said. "Honest, it drives me nutty. Now, of all times!"

"Really, Mr. Maney, I don't see how you can make a joke of a thing like this," Mrs. Madison protested. "Someone tried to kill us!"

"Well, now I'll tell you," Maney said, "that might be it and again it might not."

"Only a madman would do such a thing, Jack," Harry Dexter said, speaking for the first time. The blacksmith was in his mid-forties, with thinning hair and the long, hollowed-out look of a man with ulcers.

"You're so right, Harry, honey," Slim said eagerly. "Some screwball!"

"You figure it that way, Harry?" Maney asked. "He was after the whole mob?"

"Well, I don't know. I suppose so," said Dexter, rubbing his toes thoughtfully.

"Tell me something, Harry. Can you think of anyone who might want to knock you off?"

"That's ridiculous, Jack!"

"Can you?"

"No."

"Mrs. Madison? How about you?"

Almost imperceptibly Mrs. Madison tossed her head. "Certainly not!"

"How about it, Doc?" Maney asked, bending over Wren. "Got any enemies?"

The supine dentist shivered. "N-no."

"Well, there you see, Mrs. Madison. I'm the only one with enemies and I'm not worried." He was pleased by the idea.

"But..."

"Just suppose it was some hophead who followed us down here and locked the door," Maney went on. "Sure, we want to find him and lock him up. But he's not so dangerous. He's not going around shooting up the place. If we start yelling murder to everyone the papers are bound to get hold of it. Just imagine what the papers could do with what happened here tonight. What would the papers do, Joe?"

"Go to town?" Bateman offered.

"No, no, no," Maney protested, "I mean the headlines, lad."

"Sorry," said Joe and frowned. "Four Found in Food Freezer, Foulplay Feared?"

"And?"

Concentrating, Bateman began to pace the floor. "Blond Beauty Grilled in Icebox Caper ... Socialites Mum on Orgy Charge."

"Joe!" Slim said. "This isn't an orgy, they're square dancing upstairs!"

"Who'll believe *that?*" he snapped back. "'No Enemies,' Says Mrs. J. Parker Madison, Son Held."

"Stop it!" said Mrs. Madison. She was blushing.

"That just gives you an idea," Maney said. "If there's anything a Boston paper likes to get its teeth into it's something like this. I could keep it out of some of them but not all of them." Again he turned to Jupiter. "What do you think?"

"I'm not thinking. I'm just watching. You're the victims."

"Exactly!" said Mrs. Madison. "I'm going to get Chief Howland. Come along Tom!"

Tom hesitated and then, catching Jupiter's eye, he shrugged and followed his mother up the stairs.

Harry Dexter said, "I think she's right, Jack. You can't have a thing like this happen and just do nothing about it."

Maney tipped up the bottle, sighed, and wiped his mouth with the back of his hand. He picked up the colorful jacket Mrs. Madison had left on a chair and put it on. "If the dancing is going to stop maybe you'd better get back to the bar, lad."

"Check, Boss," Joe said and went upstairs.

Dr. Wren got to his feet, smiled vaguely, and found a chair.

"Feeling okay, Doc?" Maney asked.

Wren nodded. "Dizzy for a moment. Fine now." He took off his glasses and began to wipe them carefully with his handkerchief.

It was an odd scene and, with the arrival of Howland, would become odder. Howland L. Howland, in his capacity of real estate agent, had been Jupiter's first contact with the town but he had never seen him in action as Chief of Police. The Saxon force consisted of two constables and half a dozen special officers, all, including Howie, appointed by the board of selectmen. The demand for law enforcement was ordinarily not great and a policeman in uniform was a rare sight except at town meetings or other community gatherings tending to create a parking problem.

Upstairs the music stopped abruptly.

"So much for the square dancing," Maney said and looked at Slim. "Too bad, huh, sugar?"

"Those squares. Honestly!"

"She doesn't like square dancing," Maney said to Jupiter.

"I know. She told me."

"She can't understand it's all for a worthy cause. Books for the library."

"Books, shmooks." She still had her glass in her hand and now she finished off the drink.

"What a way to talk!" said Maney. "Jonesy, here, is writing a book, sugar, and he just saved my life."

"Oh, Jonesy, I'm sorry, honey!" She patted his arm. "I used to read, you know, creeps, but lately, I don't now, what's creepy? Are you writing a creep, love?"

"In a sense. Yes."

"Say, this is kind of like a creep but real, huh, Jonesy?" she suggested. "But I don't know, is it? In creeps it's glunk a character is conked off and then people slink around suspectin' each other. What's to that? This way, I don't know, it's friendly."

Both Dexter and Wren were watching her,

fascinated. Maney, smiling slightly, lit a cigarette and then Chief Howland arrived.

With him, in the order named, were Mrs. Madison, Mrs. Wren, Mrs. Dexter, and, somewhat surprisingly, Mrs. Jones. Betty, her hair wind-blown from her recent exertions, cocked an eyebrow at Jupiter from the stairs. Mrs. Wren went directly to her husband and, standing in front of him, clicked her tongue. "I've been looking everywhere for you, John!"

"I'm quite all right, my dear."

Dot Dexter, unsure of how seriously the whole affair was being taken, stood silently at Harry's side while he put on his shoes. Howland took a stand near the freezer door and wiped his expansive face with a blue bandanna handkerchief. "Sweats a man, callin'," he announced and Jupiter realized he had decided to adopt his rustic role for the occasion. It was an accent and delivery he employed on his urban house-seeking prospects, directing their attention from doubtful timbers to salable lilac-ed vistas. Maney held out the bottle to him. "Short snort, Chief, before getting down...to work?"

Howland shook his head. "Now then, folks, what's all the shoutin' about, as the feller says?"

"I've already told you what happened, Howie," Mrs. Madison said, impatiently.

"Well, ma'am, you have an' you hain't. The only information I have in my possession at the present time is you folks come down here to have a look at these here frozen birds an' while you're in there gazin' at 'em the door somehow gits itself locked. Who got you out?"

"Mr. Jones."

"And Mrs. Maney," said Jupiter.

"How'd y'know they was in there? Hear 'em shoutin' and poundin'?"

"No," said Jupiter. He decided Howie was having too good a time. "I should say they were discovered by a process of elimination combined with a touch of extrasensory perception."

"Well, sir, anything's good if it works. You'd bin lookin' for 'em, then?"

"They had been sought singly but it was only when Mrs. Maney recalled that they had, as a group, gone to visit the freezer that the possibility of their still being together suggested itself."

Howland observed Jupiter for a moment with his small, shrewd eyes. Then, rubbing his palm along his cheek, he said, "Y'say Mrs. Maney knew they was comin' down here, knew they was missin', an' didn't git around to lookin' in here for a whole hour?"

Both Maney and Slim started to speak but Jupiter said quickly, "I wasn't attempting to give you that impression, Chief. Mrs. Maney had been looking for her husband. She'd looked in the main house and the stable. She hadn't looked in here because the light in this room had been turned off, presumably by whoever locked the freezer door."

Howie thought this over. "Bin turnin' it over in yer head a good bit, ain't you?"

24

"Some," Jupiter admitted.

"Y'think it was a real, honest to Gawd killin' try?"

"It could be. Another hour would have done, I believe," he bowed slightly to Maney, "the trick. The difficulty at the moment is not who-dunit but who got done, unless, of course, we should be dealing with the work of an indiscriminate, psychopathic killer. Assuming we are not, we must contend with a motivation for murder powerful enough to account for the cold-blooded disposal of three extra, presumably uninvolved, victims."

"Whew!" said Howland and elaborately used his bandanna again.

Betty moved across the room to Jupiter's side and whispered, "It's been a long, long time." She was referring, he knew, to his regrettable record as an amateur sleuth. It was a sporadic involvement with murder, stretching back nearly fifteen years, which he had tried to account for by chance but which he now admitted must stem from an unconscious channeling of his normal predilection for violence into this one special field. Much as the banker must bank or the preacher preach, he, Edmund Jones, had been grotesquely conditioned to deduce amateurishly. For nearly six years it had been suppressed but now, trembling, he felt the old urge surge overwhelmingly. Betty touched his arm in a gesture of both understanding and reassurance. "We'll manage," she whispered and winked.

Howland had begun to massage his jaw again, looking at Maney. "I see y'got a game leg, Mister Maney."

"You're observant," Maney said, not smiling. "My wife shot me four days ago, as well you know."

"Didn't know. Only heard. Ain't there a law sez y'got to report a gunshot wound to the police?"

"I believe there is. This particular wound was examined by the Attorney General and the Governor of the State. They got a great laugh out of it."

Howland, looking a bit desperate, tried a smile. "Reckon if it's good enough for them two it's good enough for me."

"I hope so." It was apparent they were observing a side of Jack Maney that had been useful in his business career. "One more thing, Howland. If you should happen to get any more *idées* like this in that small-town head of yours, don't let them out."

Because of the normal crimson state of his face, it was impossible to tell if Howland was blushing. "Bin a crime committed here, Mister Maney. Got a right to do my job."

Ignoring him, Maney snapped on a wall switch and beckoned to Jupiter. "Got a new tractor out here I'd like you to see. Come on."

Curious, Jupiter followed him out into the

garage end of the basement. Maney actually did have a new tractor and he climbed up on its seat and gripped the wheel. "Funny thing," he said, "ever since I was a kid I've been a pushover for tractors. Hard to explain. Jonesy, lad, I have this feeling it was little ol' Slim who locked the door."

Jupiter allowed himself a few seconds to assimilate this thought. "Why?"

"You mean why do I think so or why would she do it?"

"Either, I guess."

"I won't get burned if you say what you think, Jonesy. I wasn't mad at Howie just now, just tossing a scare into him before he got out of line with this thing. The point is if it got out she locked us in there, it would be kind of tough on her around here. You know how people talk in a little town like this."

Jupiter could find no trace of amusement in Maney's face. "Are you serious?"

"Never more."

"Are you asking me if I think your wife tried to kill you and three other people just now?"

"Oh, my Lord!" Maney slapped the side of his head. "Well, I can see how you might get it like that, after all. Hell, no! No, you see she was there when we went downstairs and she didn't like the party and I figure she might have locked us in to stir things up. She has no idea how dangerous a thing like that could be!"

"Oh," said Jupiter. "What's stopping you

from going to her and asking? Putting it up to her, man to wife?"

"She'd never admit it. Never. She still claims she shot me by accident."

"She didn't?"

"Not a chance. Why, you can line up a dozen aspirin tablets at fifty feet, hand her a .22 automatic and, pop, pop, pop, she'll powder every one. I've seen her do it. Joe'll tell you."

Jupiter sighed. "Texas must be a wonderful place."

"She didn't learn that in Texas. Her old man is a druggist in Waco and she never saw a gun until she got to Broadway. She went around with a kid in the Army for a while. He was nuts about shooting galleries and they had themselves a hell of a time."

Out of the corner of his eye Jupiter had seen a movement behind the truck in the shadows at the end of the basement. He could see nothing there now and he decided it had been a rat or a bat or his imagination.

Maney pulled up his pant leg and pointed to a small bandage on his calf. "See how she creased me, lad? Half an inch one way and she'd have missed, an inch the other and she'd have busted my leg. That was no accident!" He said it proudly.

Jupiter looked back quickly at the truck but saw nothing. "Was she bored with the rat hunt?"

Maney laughed. "She was mad. We were ar-

guing about the score. We'd given her a proba-
ble but she claimed a kill. Said she could see the
dead rat lying out there so I went to look. It was
dead all right and I was holding it up by the tail
when she shot me. Said the gun went off by
mistake." He laughed again shortly. "It's quite a
sport, Jonesy, you ought to come along with us
some night. There're not so many rats, but you
get a shot now and then. We have the truck
rigged up with deck chairs and we sit there
drinking and lying to each other and it's not
uncomfortable on a good moonlight night
when the wind's right. What's the matter?"

There had been another movement and this
time Jupiter could definitely distinguish a man's
foot sticking out behind the rear wheel of the
truck.

He nodded in that direction. "We've got company."

3

Maney swung around on the seat of the tractor and the intruder stepped out into the light, revealing himself to be Arnold, the Indian. He was a short, wiry man in work clothes and he seemed sheepish and relatively sober.

"Well, Arnold," Maney said, after looking at him for some time. "What are you doing out here?"

Arnold grinned, exhibiting a fine set of broken teeth. "I been a bad Indian tonight."

Although it was popularly supposed that Arnold could catch trout with his bare hands and locate water with a witch-hazel stick there was always a debate when his name came up about the amount of Indian blood in his veins. Arnold himself maintained he was a direct descendant of Massasoit and it was undeniable that he could pass on a reservation, but one local authority had dogmatically stated that he had about as much Indian blood as the percentage of alcohol to be found in a tearoom Tom Collins. From there the debate raged.

"What have you been up to?"

"Oh, I've taken strong liquor and looked the young girls up and down something fearful. I should be ashamed."

"There aren't any young girls down here," Maney said sharply. "What are you doing in here?" He climbed down from the tractor.

Arnold stood his ground. Harassed baby sitters had been caught shouting, "Arnold, the Indian, will getcha if you don't behave!" but Jupiter doubted if this had ever added much to the traumatic experience of their charges. Arnold was hardly sinister. He did odd jobs around town and fulfilled his prime function by playing up to his reputation as the leading "character" in Saxon. He regularly received one or two write-in votes for selectman and this was good for a yearly laugh.

"Come on, tell me," Maney said and walked down to the truck.

"Well, now," Arnold said, "I'd better tell you the truth about it. I come down here with the idea to pinch a couple of them plump young birds out of your freezer."

"That's what I thought."

"You'd never have missed 'em but I'm ashamed all the same. It's the strong liquor gets hold of me."

Maney smiled. "Do you really feel guilty about it, Arnold?"

"I do indeed."

"Are you a big enough man to forgive yourself?"

Pleased with the way things were going, Arnold pondered this while he scratched his head. "Well, now. If you was to forgive me it's likely I could see my way clear to letting myself off."

"Good. Now tell me how long you were listening at that door."

Arnold slapped his thigh. "You're a sharp one! By God, I respect a sharp man!"

"How long?" Maney snapped it out, not fooling any more.

Arnold licked his lips. "Some minutes, I suspect."

Maney grunted, beckoned to Jupiter, and pointed into the back of the truck. "This is the rat rig I was telling you about, Jonesy."

On the truck were two brightly striped canvas chairs, a white metal table, a standard size icebox, and on the floor a worn but serviceable Oriental rug.

"The rug is a nice touch," Jupiter admitted.

"Joe's idea. If you must live, he believes, live right." He looked at the Indian. "Arnold, I think you ought to go and have a little talk with Howie."

Arnold looked unhappily at his feet and Jupiter felt a sudden sympathy for him. There was a hard, possibly vicious quality close to the surface of Maney's affability he had not noticed before tonight.

"You upset about them two little birds I didn't get?"

"No, but I've been thinking about those birds. Now if I'd been planning to take them out of the freezer, I'd have made sure there was no light on in that room and nobody in it before I came way around through here to get at 'em. See what I mean, Arnold?"

"No, I can't say I do."

"I've got this feeling," Maney said, "maybe you weren't after any birds at all. I'd like to find out what you were after."

"I tell ya I was after birds! I don't know about no light. I come around back in here an' up to that door an' that's when I see a light an' hear folks talkin'! God damn you rich bastids, you never believe a poor man when he's tellin' the truth!"

Arnold spat close to Maney's toes but the big man didn't move or speak.

"You think I locked that God damn door? What have I got 'gainst you an' them others I'd do a thing like that?"

"I don't think you locked the door," Maney said quietly, "but I do think you protest too much."

"Don't know what you mean by that." Suddenly a crafty look came into Arnold's eyes. "S'posing...just s'posing now, I was to go in there and say to Howland I seen you folks going into that room 'bout an hour ago and I seen your wife coming out. How'd that set with you?"

Maney observed him for a moment and then, surprisingly, he laughed. "By God, Arnold, you're a swift one! How come you never made a dollar for yourself?"

The crafty look remained but the Indian uttered a short, man-to-man obscenity.

"The trouble with blackmail," Maney went on, still chuckling, "is you've got to have facts. Now, I know you didn't see Slim come out of there. You're a lying Indian, aren't you, Arnold?"

"Maybe. Maybe not."

"We'll go along and talk to Howland. Tell him about the birds if you want but no lies about my wife. Remember that, Arnold."

Maney put out his hand to take his arm but suddenly the Indian twisted away from him and ran out the garage door, disappearing at once in the dark. Maney made no move to go after him.

"Now I wonder why he did that?" he mused and leaned back against the truck. "What do you think, Jonesy? Do you think he saw Slim come out of there? Do you think he was really planning to hook a couple of pheasants?"

"You've got me," Jupiter said. "Are you going to tell Howland about him?"

"I don't know. Right now I'd give a hundred to one Slim locked us in but I'd like to be sure."

"I think you're wrong. If Arnold had really seen her, he wouldn't have run off."

"But, my God, man, if Slim didn't do it we've got a murderer loose!" It was apparently the first time he had seriously entertained this idea. "Hell, wouldn't one of us know if someone was trying to kill us?"

"You'd think so," Jupiter admitted. "Tell me something. How'd you four happen to get into the freezer in the first place? Were you all sitting together upstairs?"

"We were watching the dancing. Mrs. Madison had never been out here before and I offered to show her around. Harry and the Doc decided to come along too. Slim stayed upstairs."

"How did you get down there? Did you go outside or down the inside stairs?"

"The stairs."

"Did you go straight into the freezer?"

"No. I showed them the incubator and the brooder room and then we came out here and had a look at the tractor. They got the complete tour."

"Then the light was on in that room for a few minutes anyway before you went into the freezer. Somebody outside could have seen you."

Maney nodded and then smiled. "I heard you were a detective, Jonesy. Are you going to work on this thing?"

"If you want me to. It's just a hobby, a form of self-expression."

"I guarantee you'll be wasting your time. Slim locked us in."

"Maybe I can find out if she did. How long were you in the freezer before you found the door was locked?"

"Not long. Hell, I never figured the door was locked. I thought the damned hasp had snapped over and caught somehow. The door closes automatically, you know." He rubbed his chin. "I never liked the idea of that padlock but Joe wanted it. He's a nut about his birds and he was really burned last year after the dance when some of them were missing."

"How long has the lock been on there?"

"Only a couple of weeks. Maybe it was Arnold who pinched the birds last year. Wait'll Joe hears about it!" He put his hand on Jupiter's arm and they started back toward the packaging room. "Get Slim alone, Jonesy, and see what you can get out of her. She thinks you're quite a boy and maybe she'll admit it to you where she wouldn't to me or Joe."

"What happens if she admits it?"

"Well, hell, that's the end of it."

"Don't you tell the others?"

"Oh, sure, I could explain it to them, I guess. Nobody got hurt. But I don't want anything in the papers and I don't want Howland nosing around."

"Well, I'll see what I can do."

It was, he decided, a weird situation. He was engaged in what amounted to a murder investigation in which the unharmed victims unanimously denied having enemies. Unless Slim actually had locked the door, someone must be lying and his problem was to discover the victim!

The difficulty must have occurred to Howland, because he had already gone back upstairs, apparently in disgust. Mrs. Madison had followed him and the Wrens were preparing to go home.

"What's the status?" Maney asked.

"I don't think you had any right to walk off like that, Jack," Dexter complained. "How can Howland be expected to get anywhere if you don't co-operate?"

"Oh, don't be silly, Harry," Dot said. "Jack has a right to do what he wants about it. He was in there as long as you were."

"Mrs. Madison is goin' to draw for the television now," Slim explained. "I'm goin' to win it, I just know!"

Mrs. Wren, holding her husband's arm, said, "We've had a very nice time, Mr. Maney. I mean, well . . ."

"Going so soon?" Maney asked.

"Yes, I think we'd better."

"Getting late, you know," said the doctor. "Past my bedtime."

"Drop in again, Doc," Maney offered, "when we're not having a murder."

Wren smiled and bowed formally to Slim. "Good night, Mrs. Maney."

"Good night, honey," Slim said. "Take care of yourself."

The doctor might have had two drinks or a full quart under his belt for all Jupiter could tell, but from the way his wife was hustling him off it was probably the latter. He decided to walk out to their car with them and nudged Betty to follow him.

Outside Mrs. Wren said, "Well, I never! So that's the famous Jack Maney!"

"Haven't you ever met him before?" Jupiter asked.

"Never like that! Of course, I've seen them around town but...And his wife! Of course, she's very beautiful but..."

"Now, dear," Wren protested mildly.

"I'm going to get you home and into a hot tub! Why, you might have caught pneumonia!"

"I might have been dead."

"John!" She hurried him toward the car and sniffed. "I must say I don't think Howie is going to get very far trying to find out who locked you in there. Why, he hardly seemed interested!"

She climbed into the driver's seat and Wren, apparently accustomed to the arrangement, trudged around to the other side. They said good night and as the car swung around in the driveway its headlights momentarily picked up

Arnold, the Indian, standing motionless among the parked cars.

Betty had also noticed him. "What's Arnold doing around here?"

"Pheasant hunting, he says." He explained about finding him and also about the possibility of Slim's strange practical joke. "What does your womanly intuition report on that?"

"Could she have done it?"

"She shot Jack last week with a rifle. On purpose, he claims. I don't know about locking them in, though Maney's certain she did."

"Can't someone ask her?"

"I'm going to ask her but it's got to be done just right, apparently. I plan to get her out here in the moonlight and eventually, when she's in the proper mood, I'll inquire."

"Well, it's a nice night for it." She took his arm and they walked slowly back to the barn. "Do you hanker after her, dear? I thought I noticed you looking at her rather hungrily."

"Hungrily? I have to fight myself to keep from drooling. I wouldn't be surprised if it took me four or five nights to clear up this business."

"I'll tell you what I'll do. I want to help so I'll ask her myself, right now."

"Not on your life! You got me over here tonight and now I'm going to enjoy myself."

She giggled. "I meant to speak about that. I saw you out there on the floor. My!"

"I'll tell you something about square dancing," he said, the memory of his experience still bitter. "It was revived by Henry Ford and now it's being pushed by the Communists. It's the new miracle narcotic for the masses. You're a reactionary at heart."

"I know. It's because I'm a mother."

At the main door of the barn Tom Madison and Ginny Garrett, Tom's girl, were standing together and Jupiter stopped to speak to them. Ginny was the daughter of Max Garrett who, until his death two years ago, had run Garrett's General Store in Saxon. Ginny had left a department store job in Boston and come back to take over her father's business. Max had handled everything from guns to butter but Ginny had eliminated the grocery line entirely, sold out most of the other stock at auction, and laid in a line of smart tweeds, gaudy flannel shirts, imported sweaters and the like, and reprinted the old sign in antique lettering to read:

THE GENERAL STORE
Est. 1872
V. Garrett, Prop.

At Ginny's you could buy a hooked rug, a copper cocktail shaker in the form of a milk can, red flannel underwear, snuff, a painting by any one of five local artists, a coonskin cap, or one of Harry Dexter's weather vanes. Although her father had put in central heating years before, Ginny set up a potbellied stove at the back of the store and had it glowing on cold winter days. She retained one of his old glass show-cases in which she displayed a variety of old-fashioned penny candies. With Tom's help, she put out a mail order catalogue and although she had yet to do a volume of business as great as her father her mark-up would have warmed his heart. She lived alone over the store in an apartment equipped with modern blond furniture and Venetian blinds. But in spite of all this, Jupiter had heard that Mrs. Madison had recently spoken of her as "Tom's bright little townie."

"I want to thank you for saving Mother's life," Tom said. "With that light out down there we might never have found them in time."

"It was luck as much as anything."

"Harry said another hour and they would surely have been dead." Ginny shuddered. "Golly, but it's a horrible thing to think about."

Tom put his arm around her shoulders. "Never mind, darling. It's all right. Nothing happened to them."

"But you just can't stop thinking about it," she protested. "If someone really tried to kill them, why...well, what's going to happen now?"

"We're not sure someone actually tried to kill them," Tom said.

Jupiter was curious. "How would you account for it otherwise?"

"Well, I don't know. Couldn't someone have

happened along while they were in there and, well, just locked the door for safekeeping?"

"Who?" Jupiter asked. "Joe? Slim? If you saw a light on in a room outside a freezer would you lock the freezer door without looking inside? And forget to turn off the light inside? That's impossible, Tom, and you know it."

"But, dammit, Jupe, who'd want to kill those four people just like that?"

"No one," Ginny said. "If it was...murder, then, well, then, there was only one victim. That's the way it would have to be. The others were just innocent bystanders. Don't you think so?"

"That's what I think," Jupiter admitted.

Tom frowned. "Do you think it could have been Jack? Who was the victim I mean?"

"Why Maney?" Jupiter asked.

"But, my gosh, Jupe, no one would want to kill Harry or Dr. Wren or...or Mother!"

Jupiter said nothing. Undoubtedly when the news got around, as it soon would, the town would agree with Tom. For a time, at least.

"I wish we knew," Ginny said. "If we knew who it was...I mean one definite person, then at least it would limit...suspicion."

"Yes," Jupiter agreed. "It would do that all right. You know what I'd do right now if I'd been locked up in there?"

"What?"

"I'd make peace with my enemies."

He left them and went along inside to the

bar. Already the crowd was aware that something had gone wrong; people had moved into groups, their voices subdued. The Maneys and the Dexters were at a table together but before joining them Jupiter sought Joe's attention.

Joe leaned across the bar. "You know something, Jonesy? There may be more in this than meets..."

With a stubby forefinger he pulled down the lid of one eye.

4

It was nearing two and although the party was officially over it had assumed a character closer to Slim's heart. The "screwballs," perhaps twenty-five, who remained appeared to be adequately "likkered up" and the "swing your partners, loopy-do" had given way to normal dancing to the "smoochy" rhythms of Joe Bateman at the piano. As yet Jupiter had been unable to get her away for what he had come to call his "little talk" but he still had hopes. Earlier he had very nearly succeeded in luring her to the stable for this purpose but just then Mrs. Madison had announced the drawing on the television set. Nor did it strike him as particularly astonishing, in view of the evening itself, that the winner turned out to be Mrs. Jack Maney.

"I knew it! I knew it!" she called when Mrs. Madison, a bit unhappily, read out the name on the ticket.

There had been a short silence during which

Maney had whispered to his wife but this had been broken by a loud "Like hell I will! I won it and it's mine!" from Slim. This was received with laughter and hearty, though not overwhelming, applause.

The bar had closed for an hour to empty the hall but was open now on a serve-yourself basis, the drinks being free. "We've bought enough books for one night," Maney had said. Tom had driven his mother home but had returned and remained with Ginny. A good number of the late stayers were, like Tom and Ginny, young and unmarried, although there was a strong showing of hardy veterans like the Joneses and the Dexters who knew a good thing when they saw it. The lights had been dimmed, smoke abounded, and it would have been difficult to tell that a murder attempt, if indeed it was that, had been made.

"By God, she's a refreshing thing," Harry Dexter said. He had been standing silently at the bar with his pipe and Jupiter assumed the remark was addressed to him. He followed the blacksmith's line of sight and saw he was observing Slim, draped elegantly against the piano and singing softly and slightly off key.

"Uh, huh." He realized that Dexter, known locally as a man who could hold his liquor, was well along and was about to embark on some theme close to his heart.

"Natural as a child and with a child's unaffected grace."

Aware that the Dexters had no children Jupiter decided not to remark how early in life most children lost their unaffected grace.

"God, what beauty! It shines through her like a torch!"

Looking stealthily at his companion Jupiter was suddenly convinced that Dexter was in love with Slim and had reached the point where it was necessary to tell someone about it. Ordinarily he would have made at least a half-hearted attempt to stem the confession but this time he excused his silence on the grounds that Dexter was a potential victim and therefore fair game for investigation.

"Dorothy's terribly inhibited. Terribly tense. That's one reason we moved from New York, you know. I hoped out here, closer to realities, would be better for her. It's helped some but not enough." Dexter looked away from Slim to the dance floor and pointed with the stem of his pipe. "Look at her now."

Dot Dexter, with her eyes closed, was dancing fondly with a youth Jupiter knew only by sight. At the moment she seemed neither inhibited nor tense but he knew what Dexter was talking about.

"That kind of thing used to drive me half crazy but now, and this is God's truth, I feel only pity for her."

In an effort to break up the conversation Jupiter turned to his own wife, who was saying to Maney, "All right, here's another. Bases full, two out, three and two on the batter. What's the pitch?"

"The big one," said Maney promptly. "Or the payoff pitch."

"What else?"

"All the runners will go on this one. You make 'em too easy, sweetheart. Now here's one . . ."

Dexter touched Jupiter's arm and reluctantly he turned back.

"Tell me something, strictly in private, Jones," Harry said in a low voice. "Do you think Maney's in love with his wife?"

Jupiter considered and rejected a number of answers to this question. Finally he said, "I wonder if this discussion is getting us anywhere, Harry."

Dexter sucked on his pipe, giving no indication of what he thought of this answer. Jupiter was briefly troubled by a sense of having failed an acquaintance in need but he had found it necessary, in recent years, to sift his personal commitments and he felt that Harry's dilemma, troubling as it was, failed to rate a priority on his time or emotions. He had discovered he took personal relationships more seriously than most and was learning to pace himself accordingly. This was true also of his social responsibilities. There were thoughtful men in the town, including Dexter, who believed in and worked for what he called the Small Town Idea —a belief that social problems must be worked out on the grass roots level if they were ever to be adjusted on a national or international scale. He acknowledged that his own objections to this thought might be invalid but they prevented him from taking any more than a token part in the activities of the town. Thus he missed the satisfactions of tangible group accomplishment as well as, he was ready to admit, a good deal of plain hard work. His energies were employed on his book, his children, small household projects, and a limited amount, like tonight, of social drinking.

Dexter got up suddenly and cut in on Dot. To forestall the possibility that he might be planning to bring her back for some more uncomfortable talk, Jupiter went to the piano. Slim put her arm around his shoulder, commanded him to sing, and he dutifully accompanied her to the end of the song.

"You have a request, sir?" Joe asked, playing chords. "Some nostalgic tune from your memory book?"

"'Stardust,'" said Jupiter.

"Ah, yes," said Joe, going into it. "Well, I remember the day I wrote this one. I was in Buffalo, living half-starved in a garret room, when out of the blue..."

"Come on, Jonesy," Slim said. "Let's say good night to my lovely."

Following her out to the stable he suspected she had seen through his simple ruse but he was mistaken; she had something on her own mind she wanted to discuss.

"Honey," she said, after the ritual of fondling the sleepy Stardust had been taken care of, "I saw you talking to Harry and I just know he was talking about me. What am I going to do about that poor dear man?"

Jupiter mentally tossed up and the decision came down to play it dumb. "What do you mean, Slim?"

"Jonesy, do people really fall in love, the way it says in books?"

This discussion would be interminable, he decided, if they both played it dumb so he abruptly switched his tactics. "Are you trying to decide whether to sleep with him or not?"

"Jonesy! What a way to talk! Yes, honey, I guess I am."

"Well, don't ask me to be an accomplice to adultery, Slim. I have my code and it's extremely rigid on that point."

She didn't like this and her jaw went out.

"I like you because you're serious and you know things, Jonesy, so don't make jokes when I'm serious and want to know something. Okay?"

"Okay," he said, chastened. "What do you really want to know?"

"Like I asked you before, do people really fall in love the way they say? So it hurts them and things like that?"

"Haven't you ever been in love that way, Slim?"

"Uh, uh. Honest. Never."

"What about you and Jack?"

Her eyes widened. "But, honey, Jack and I like each other! We have fun!"

Jupiter laughed outright, shaking his head.

"That's all right, isn't it? There's nothing wrong with that, is there?" she demanded, frowning.

"No. That's wonderful, Slim."

"But about Harry. Do you think he means all the things he says?"

"I don't know what he says but I have a strong hunch he means them." He cleared his throat and swallowed. "Love is a pretty complicated affair, Slim. That's why there's so much about it in books. As a simple rule you might say only troubled people fall in love. People who have doubts and are unsure about themselves." She was listening intently and it occurred to him that this was perhaps the weirdest lecture he had ever given—and he had delivered some odd ones at Harvard. "A person in love sees qualities in the other he'd like to see in himself. As children we're taught to admire the standard virtues but few of us manage to grow up and practice all of them. The old conscience begins to act up and we fall for someone we believe has the missing virtue still intact. At least that's a theory and if it's right it makes love a Good Thing."

"Gee! Well, all I know is an awful lot of sad characters have fallen in love with me."

"I'm not surprised. But they were probably pretty nice guys, weren't they?"

"Like Harry, most of them were sweet. But, hey, what does that make me?"

"It makes you well adjusted to the point of abnormality, Slim. Take Harry. As a boy he was told he should stand on his own two feet and look after his interests in life. Be a man. He was also told he should be kind to animals and people. Turn the other cheek. Kindness got the upper hand. It's not this simple but he's in love with you because he believes you're a very tough chicken indeed. He's right, incidentally."

"Uh, huh. I guess I'm tough enough, Jonesy. But honestly what am I going to do about him?"

"What did you do about the others?"

"Oh, them. Well, that was before Jack. I mean . . . well, I let them down easy, I guess that is what I did. I always felt so sorry for them, they were so goony. My!" She was silent for a moment, reviewing her memories. "Then it's not just an act with Harry?"

"No, I think not."

"Well, I'm glad to find that out anyway. You know, Jonesy, a girl like me gets an awful lot of propositions. Honest, you'd be amazed!"

"I might, at that."

"The *people!*" She shook her head at the range of male audacity she had encountered.

Then she sighed. "But Harry wants to marry me."

"As long as he keeps it on that basis you're safe enough. Just don't encourage him by taking shots at Jack."

"Oh, I'll never do that again! That was an awful thing. Did you ever have a gun go off when you didn't mean it to?"

"Is that what happened, Slim?"

She nodded. "It was funny except not really. Jack was out there holding this old rat up by the tail and I thought I'll just shoot it out of his hand and surprise him. So I pointed the gun and then I thought, oh, my, I might miss and hit him in the hand, so I brought the gun down and that's when it went off and hit him in the leg."

Jupiter considered this version of the story for a minute. "Didn't you tell him that was what happened?"

"Oh, yes, I told him just what happened because I knew he wouldn't believe me. He thinks I did it on purpose."

"I don't quite get that," Jupiter said, running one hand through his hair.

"Well, honey, I wouldn't want him to think I was careless! Not with a gun! It was just plain dumb lucky for me I hit him in the leg like I did."

The only course, he decided, was to suspend judgment on the rat incident. "About this freezer business, Slim. This could get messy and complicated for all the people involved."

"Oh, I know that, Jonesy!" Again her eyes were wide in, perhaps, innocent wonder. "I just don't see how a person could do a thing like that! Not even in fun!"

"Do you think anyone might have done it in fun?"

She nodded. "Except not leaving them that long. That was too long to leave them for a joke, honey."

"That's what I think."

"I wish you'd try and find out who did it, Jonesy. I don't think that fat Howland ever will. You're so smart...you know, you read so many books and stuff...I'll bet you could find out who did it if you just tried." She frowned. "I'll tell you what. You find out and I'll give you the television set. You don't have one in your house, do you?"

He shook his head, as much in wonder as in answer. "I'll tell you a secret, Slim. I love you."

"Like Harry or just for laughs?"

"For laughs."

"Then that's all right. You can kiss me if you want, Jonesy."

With every intention of keeping it on a high, neighborly plane, he complied but discovered at once the impossibility of kissing her in that fashion. He had stumbled, apparently, onto her personal form of artistic expression.

"There now," she said, releasing him at last.

She linked her arm with his and led him from the stable. "I always thought you were okay, Jonesy, but I wanted to make sure."

He decided he was getting nowhere at all with the case. True, he was having a pretty good time but perhaps now he should go home and tackle it in the morning with a relatively clear head. Like Arnold he could forgive himself; he was human and alcohol and Slim didn't mix.

5

Jupiter awoke to a warm spring sunrise, a plethora of bird calls, and the sibilant cries of his children warning each other not to wake Daddy and Mummy. He lay still for a time following the sudden scurryings past the door, the small crashes of falling objects, and the short, sharp screams of agony, then he got up and cornered them in the bathroom. They were Susan, seven, Mark, five, and Ricky, three, all in varying degrees of dampness and undress.

"I've got a surprise for you," he said, staring down their quick suspicion. "If you'll get yourselves dressed you can have a picnic. A breakfast picnic outdoors. You can make whatever you want to eat."

They communed silently together, studying the proposition.

"Whatever we want?" Susan asked and, when he nodded, "Marshmallow and peanut butter sandwiches?"

Jupiter swallowed. "Yes."

"'oot beer?" Mark asked.

"I said whatever you want!"

"My Gawd," said Ricky, employing his latest overworked witticism.

Jupiter took two aspirin and slipped back into bed.

"Thank you, dear," Betty murmured.

"I knew you were awake. You can't fool me."

"M'mm," she said.

They slept for two hours in relative peace.

Later, at breakfast in the kitchen, Betty said, "There's just one thing. How much hanky panky went on between you two in the stable?"

"What a question," he said and sipped his coffee.

"Now I know. Well, I can't say I blame you. She's a wieldy item."

"She is indeed. You know it's a horrid thing to admit but I've been faithful to you all these years on simple, moral grounds."

"Oh, that's all right. I don't care how you rationalize it as long as it works. Do you think she locked that door?"

"She might have. If she didn't it's bound to get nasty. Those people were more or less in a state of shock last night. I have an idea my services are going to be in demand today. Say, fellers, how would you like a television set?"

The children had returned from their picnic and were dawdling about the kitchen, pretending to be uninterested in the adult conversation.

"Did you win it, Daddy? Did you?" Susan asked, excited.

"No. Mrs. Maney won it but she's going to give it to me if I solve the mystery."

Their eyes narrowed warily. "Reegy?" Mark demanded.

"Really. This is a real mystery and I'm the detective."

"Murduh!" said Ricky, a radio listener.

"Not yet," said Jupiter and explained to them what had happened the night before. "So I'm going to be busy thinking and finding out things all day and you're not to bother me."

"Do it, Daddy," Susan ordered. "Oh, boy, television!"

"Right after breakfast I'm going to the village and start to work," he announced, a cautious eye on Betty.

"Can we go?"

"Certainly not. You stay home with your mother."

"Hah!" said Betty from the sink.

Driving the two miles to town he realized he had a mild hangover accompanied by the usual twinges of remorse. But all that would pass and it was a beautiful day to be up and doing. Already householders were out and engaged in their vernal chores; here a man was at grips with a new power lawn mower, there a woman on her knees invoked her tulips. At the village common the old white houses faced each other, solid and prosperous under their ancient, blighted elms. Above them all the plain spire of the Unitarian church was a forefinger pointing straight to God.

My, my, he thought, I have got a hangover this morning.

He pulled up at the post office and toyed momentarily with the revolutionary act of not going directly in to get his mail but discarded it as a childish protest; he lived in the town and would abide by its customs.

He opened his box, withdrew his mail, and was about to shut the small door when he noticed the eye of the postmistress looking out at him from the other side.

"Good morning there, Mr. Jones," she said.

He bent down and smiled in politely at the eye. "Good morning, Mrs. Fairweather."

"I saw you drive up and I wanted to ask... they said you found them...I don't see why they weren't frozen stiff as it is but...what a terrible thing, dear me...but I wanted to ask what you thought...I mean they're saying about Mrs. Maney and that Joe...that they've been carrying on and it might have been them together...after the money..."

He straightened up quickly from the box and held his breath. It had started already then, worse than he'd expected. Mrs. Fairweather was a tiny woman, almost a dwarf, and undoubtedly had her own special need for this kind of thing. But...

"It's only what they're saying, Mr. Jones. I don't know anything myself."

He bent down again to the opening. "If you don't know anything yourself, Mrs. Fairweather, you're performing a poor service as a government employee in talking this way."

He flipped the door shut and left the post office. He had, he realized, just contracted for atrocious postal service for as long as he lived in the town but there were times when sympathy and understanding, valuable as they might be, were not enough and a stand was necessary. For three years he had avoided the necessity of stands in Saxon but now that he was committed to the case, as he seemed to be, the stands would come thick and fast. Watch out, citizens, he muttered, the wraps are coming off.

"Well! You certainly look full of purpose this morning!"

He had walked past the red-fronted chain store, the drugstore, and the package store, and had not seen Ginny Garrett standing in the doorway of her General Store. She was pretty and competent in a gingham dress.

"Hi, Ginny." He stopped and grinned sheepishly. "Yes. I find my emotions engaged at the moment."

"I guess we all do this morning. I . . . I wanted to speak to you if they're not too engaged."

"All right."

He followed her in among the quaint merchandise and sat down in a new Hitchcock chair, not a reproduction, as its tag pointed out, but a *real* Hitchcock chair manufactured in the *original* Hitchcock factory. From an electric percolator, hidden beneath the counter, Ginny poured coffee for them both. She looked a bit pale but then, he thought, I undoubtedly look pale myself.

"I don't suppose there's any word yet on this business?" she asked, and when he shook his head: "I wish it would get cleared up. You don't know Tom's mother very well, do you?"

"No."

"I guess you've heard she doesn't think much of me for a daughter-in-law. Everyone knows that. As a matter of fact I can understand how she feels. The Madisons and the Garretts have always been pretty far apart in this town. She's entitled to her standards as much as anyone else."

"That's very adult and broad-minded of you, Ginny."

"Thank you. That's not what I wanted to say, though. You know last night you said a funny thing."

"I wish I could recall it."

"You said if you'd been locked in that freezer you'd hurry up and make peace with your enemies."

"That's right. I did say that."

"Well, that's what she's done."

From a nearby counter he picked up a child's

high-heeled cowboy boot and turned it over in his hands. "How's that?"

"I'd better tell you the whole thing. Last month Tom told her he wanted to marry me and she said if he did she'd stop the money for his magazine. Not only that but she'd leave all her money when she died to charity. She'd do it, too."

"What did Tom have to say to that?"

She flushed. "He said he'd marry me anyway. You know him well enough for that, don't you?"

"I guess so, Ginny, but that's quite a wad of money."

"It certainly is. That's what I told him. But, honestly, it's not the money. It's just that if she felt so strongly about it I don't think the marriage would work. Not if we lived in this town and both of us love the town." She put down her coffee cup and stood up. "So, anyway, I said we'd better not do anything for a while and then last night happens. This will give you a little idea how that woman operates. She was waiting up for Tom when he got home last night and she said she'd been doing some thinking and she guessed she was wrong about me and it was all right for him to marry me. And then at the end she hinted, just hinted mind you, that it might have been Tom or me or both of us who locked that door!"

Jupiter said nothing for half a minute, then he put the cowboy boot carefully back in place.

"Well, you've got to admit it's ingenious. You can say that for it." He took a deep breath. "What did Tom do?"

"He left and came here and he was almost out of his head. I told him his mother was sick, that it was the shock and everything. Finally he left and went to his office. I guess he's up there now." She was close to tears. "Of course, *we* know neither of us could do a thing like that. We *know* it. But there it is. Suppose this is never cleared up?"

"It will be."

"But suppose it isn't? Don't you see what she's done? There'll always be that one chance, that one suspicion...don't you see? I'm doing it already!"

She was crying now and he got up and put his hands on her shoulders. "Listen. You know Tom didn't lock that door. He couldn't have."

"I know, I know."

"Listen to me, Ginny. Tom might try to kill his mother, no one can know about that, but he didn't lock that door. Do you want to know why I'm sure?"

She nodded, sobbing.

"Every murderer has to rationalize his murder to himself. Tom might rationalize the murder of his mother alone but never killing those three other people. He likes Wren and Maney and Dexter. It would be psychologically impossible for him to kill them. And the same is true of you. Now get yourself organized, Ginny.

You've got a big enough problem with Mrs. Madison without adding a lot of nonsense to it."

She got out a handkerchief and applied it. "Thanks. Thanks a lot. I wish you'd go and see Tom."

"I will."

He went out and stood in the sunshine, hoping what he'd told her was true.

6

The editorial office of the *Moderator* was across the street above the fire station. Jupiter climbed the outside stairs and walked in without knocking. Tom Madison was sitting at his desk, in the same clothes he'd had on the night before. The room, with its filing cabinets, stacks of back issues, and pinned-up photographs, was too orderly to look prosperous, even if he hadn't known how much money the magazine was losing.

"Hi, Jupe," Tom said dully. "I saw you come out of Ginny's. How's she feeling?"

"Better, I think." He sat down opposite Tom and put his feet up on the window sill. "Are you planning to marry her?"

"I'd like to. She's the one who's been holding things up. I guess you know how Mother's been about it."

Jupiter nodded. "Ginny tells me your mother offered some dark suggestions last night."

Tom looked away, color coming into his

cheeks. "Yeah. I always knew Mother was pretty determined but this . . . it's sort of frightening."

"I assume you're familiar with psychiatry's handy explanation of what's going on here?"

"Sure, sure. I've thought a lot about that. I'm the pampered, only child of the domineering mother from way back. I know the standard answer, too. Make a clean break, my boy. Get out on your own in the world." He laughed shortly and shook his head. Then he clenched his fist and banged the deck. "But, dammit, why should I? I love this town and I want to live in it. Take the magazine. How many guys my age in city jobs would like to swap with me? I'm in a damned good spot, don't think I don't realize it."

"With your mother accusing you of murder?"

"She doesn't believe it. She's just trying to bust things up between Ginny and me."

"She's not doing badly. You two should have been married a year ago."

"I know. I suppose it's my fault we're not. But . . . well, I hoped the magazine would catch on before I made the break with Mother."

Jupiter picked up the May issue from the desk and flipped through its slim pages.

"You may as well tell me what you think is wrong with it," Tom said. "Everyone else has."

Well, Jupiter thought, if it's going to be a day for the truth all around I might as well make the most of it.

"Your magazine's a schizoid, Tommy. You're

half hick, half slick. Look at this. Here's a scientific piece on the artificial insemination of cattle and right next to it a sly essay on amateur vegetable gardeners. I liked that one, as a matter of fact. Who's M. J. Thomas who wrote it?"

"Me," Tom said, pleased. "Those are my initials backward."

Jupiter had been convinced of this but he knew when to give a compliment as well as the next man. "Your trouble as an editor is you don't take a stand for or against an idea and stick with it. Oddly enough you're handling this magazine about the way you've handled your love life."

Tom flushed. "I don't think that's quite fair or true. I've taken a stand on Ginny and, dammit, the magazine has always stuck to one line."

"What line is that?"

"The liberal line, I guess. The main idea is that the informed urbanites, returning to the land, can and should make common purpose with the townspeople. All right, the *ignorant* townspeople, because they are ignorant of any issues beyond their noses."

Jupiter sighed. "I'll tell you something, Tom. There aren't any informed urbanites returning to the land."

"What do you mean? What about you and Harry Dexter and a dozen others, right here in Saxon?"

"We're informed and we're urbanites but we're not returning to the land. Every town in

66

New England is a suburb of a city and every city in the country is getting larger. We may grow a few vegetables, raise a few chickens, and chop some wood on weekends, but we're still as soundly urban as if there were a subway out there under Main Street."

Tom leaned forward and nodded. "That may be true. But that's not my point. I..."

"Look, Tom. What you believe in is a certain amount of government planning, a lot more decentralization of industry, the United Nations, and higher pay for teachers, and you want me and Harry Dexter to spread the gospel among the backward natives. Right?"

"Right, I guess." Tom grinned.

"So the backward native says all this is going to cost me money in taxes and the hell with it. He's right, too, up to a point. Your small town is 90 per cent middle class. And there's no immediate, visible advantage to the middle class in any move toward socialism, however watered down."

"I know it's hard to make them see it but I know it's worth the fight."

"I won't argue that. My point is you're not making a fight with this," Jupiter said and tapped the magazine. "You throw in a good word for the TVA or something similar every once in a while but that's not following a line. What's your circulation?"

"Just under five thousand."

"Well, you put on a good liberal campaign.

Slant every article in that direction and you'll have it down under a thousand in no time. On the other hand if you develop a good hate for Big Government and a strong love for private enterprise you might, with luck, break even in five years."

Tom sat back, sighed, and brushed his hands through his hair. "You may be right, I suppose I have been kidding myself. I figured it must be something wrong with the material."

"Well, frankly, old man, your material isn't so hot, either. The kind of writing you need comes high."

"Jeepers, Jupe, you're really laying it on the line this morning!"

"I've been in hiding," Jupiter said shortly. "What are you going to do about your mother?"

"What is there to do?"

"As I understand it you haven't any income of your own."

"I have a little. Not very much, but..."

"Every once in a while, Tom, I get tired of excusing people's unpleasant actions on the grounds that they can't help themselves, that they're psychologically handicapped. Where the hell do we draw the line? Do you draw the line when your mother accuses you and Ginny of trying to kill her when she knows damned well you didn't?"

Tom was unhappy. "I walked out. I don't know what else I can do."

"Why don't you go home right now and tell her you *did* lock that door and you've decided to confess to Howland?"

"I don't get it. What good would that do?"

"If you could make her believe it she'd be against your confessing, wouldn't she? She'd have to be. She doesn't want to see her son go to jail. You've got her right where you want her, my boy. You'll have to act a little but you're capable of that." He leaned across the desk. "When she starts to plead with you, put the bite on her for a sizable settlement. Call in a lawyer and get it in writing."

Tom sat back, his hands behind his head.

"I'm sorry. I'm afraid I don't care to blackmail my own mother."

"She's been blackmailing you."

"If you want to call it that, maybe she has, but...well, that's not the way I do business, Jupe."

"The meek shall inherit the earth. What's left of it." He stood up, went around the desk, and slapped Tom on the back. "Good for you. I wanted to find out how tough you are because it took a very tough character to lock that door last night. You're no longer under suspicion."

"Well, my gosh," said Tom and just then the fire horn went off, deafeningly, in the cupola over their heads. They both jumped. "I never get used to that thing," Tom said when it stopped. He opened the window and called to a man in the street. "Where is it?"

"There's no fire," said the man. "Howie Howland is missing."

7

The circumstances leading up to the sounding of the fire horn, Jupiter was able to discover, were roughly these: a lady from Boston had arrived in Saxon for a nine o'clock appointment with Howland to inspect a property advertised as follows:

GOING, GOING——

Act fast on this grand old center chimney colonial set on five landscaped acres in countrified Saxon! 5 fireplaces, many original features, 8 rooms, 2½ baths! Forced hot water heat with oil! Big barn with box stalls! All in A–1 condition! Garden, fruit trees, berry bushes! Owner leaving state, will sacrifice for quick sale at $24,000. This is a real "find"!

Exclusive
with
Howland L. Howland

But Howland, whose office was in his house, had not been there nor had the lady from Boston been able to rouse anyone. Understandably annoyed after a twenty-minute wait she had gone to the post office to inquire about him. It was Mrs. Fairweather who set the wheels in motion. Phil Gaudy, the dancing selectman, had been in the post office at the time and a whispered discussion between him and Mrs. Fairweather had taken place. Mrs. Fairweather maintained that something must surely be wrong because Howie would never pass up a chance to unload the Carter place, which had been on the market for a year and a half. Of course, Amy Howland was spending a few days with her sister on the Cape and Howie might...But, no, if Howie was up to anything he'd be more careful about it. He hadn't even been in for his mail. And after last night...

So Phil Gaudy had driven over with the lady from Boston to Howland's, had seen his car was missing, gone in, and discovered Howie hadn't slept in his bed. Gaudy was pretty upset by that time but he'd listened politely while the lady from Boston explained at some length the circumstances of her life which had led her to look for a place in the country and how in particular she had hit upon Saxon. She was very anxious to look at the Carter place and Gaudy directed her to it. Jim MacKenzie, who had bought the house in 1935 for $4800 dollars and had put no more than that into fixing it up, would, Gaudy assured her, be happy to show her around. MacKenzie was planning to retire to California when the house was sold and he had confided to Phil a week before he'd let it go for $19,000 if he got the offer. Of course, none of this extraneous information was offered to the lady from Boston by Gaudy, who believed in minding his own business.

Back at the village it became clear to the selectman that, as a town officer, he would have to act. Undoubtedly something *had* happened to Howland. It was Gaudy's instinct, as a public official, simply to wait and see what happened but when someone suggested sounding the fire alarm he didn't oppose the idea. If Howland suddenly turned up, no one could blame Gaudy for acting hysterically, and if something was really wrong the alarm would bring out a lot of people and the responsibility would pass out of his hands.

The timing of the blast on the horn was particularly effective. Those citizens who had, on this lovely Saturday morning, undertaken ambitious outdoor projects were by midmorning quite ready for an excuse to get away from them, while others, at work on their regular business, welcomed the call even more. In the country the smallest blaze is always well at tended even in the middle of the night but here everything favored an enthusiastic turn-out.

They came in cars, trucks, and on foot and, outside on the street, Jupiter heard no disappointment expressed when the nature of the alarm was disclosed.

"Howie missing? Well, now what do you think of that!"

This was said by a veteran volunteer fire fighter who, having offered it, leaned back on the hood of his car to await developments. Here was a novel situation to be approached first of all with caution. Last night's incident was well known and had already given a certain flavor to the day; now Howie's disappearance suggested the reality of violence. Gradually a kind of grim patience appeared as the popular attitude.

Jupiter had seen Dot and Harry Dexter drive up in their jeep and he walked over to them.

"Where's the fire?" Harry asked.

Jupiter outlined the situation.

"What's being done?" Harry demanded.

"Nothing as yet. I suppose in time someone will take charge and we'll get a search under way."

Harry climbed out and went off to talk to Gaudy. Although he had nothing in mind to discuss with her, Jupiter offered Dot a cigarette.

"Well," she said, exhaling after he had lit it for her. "Some doings in the little old hamlet, eh?"

He hadn't, before last night's revelations, given very much thought to the Dexters.

Harry's retreat from the complexities of his New York life had not been as successful as he had apparently hoped. He had gained a surface simplicity at the expense of bringing his larger problems out into the open. It was possible, Jupiter thought, that the narcotic value of big city stimulation was underrated; the realities of living in an insane world were more apparent the closer one got to nature. Undoubtedly both Harry and Dot were mildly disturbed personalities but they had remained together and functioned adequately in New York. That Harry should fall seriously in love with Slim Maney might be a measure of the toll the simple life was taking of their marriage.

"Do you favor excitement?" he asked.

"I like something to happen once in a while," she said. "I can work up just so much enthusiasm for changes in the weather."

"Have you tried bird walks?"

"Not yet. But Dr. Wren promised to show me the mating flight of the male woodcock and certainly *that* would be interesting."

"I always say when in doubt, complicate your life. My solution has been children."

She flushed. "I thought it was common gossip the Dexters couldn't have children."

"I haven't heard any talk of an impediment that keeps you from adopting some."

"Well, well," she said, annoyed. "I never realized you were a giver of good advice."

"I usually manage to fight back the urge but I'm in a weakened condition this morning."

He started away but she reached out and caught his arm. "Do you really think that would help?"

"I'll say this," he said. "I don't think it could hurt the children. Children are tougher than most people realize."

She released his arm. "I wasn't thinking of it that way."

"That's the way to think about it. Particularly if you want to sell Harry the idea. Charity, rather than personal salvation. Keep smiling."

He left her and walked over to a group of men that included Tom Madison, Gaudy, and Dexter. It seemed time a definite step was taken to find out what had happened to Howland.

"We were wondering if we should call the state police," Harry said.

"Let's find out if he's still in Saxon first," Jupiter suggested. "The thing to do is look for his car. If we can't find his car we won't be able to find him. We'll split the town into four sections, north, south, east, and west. Harry takes north, I'll take the south, you, Tom, can have the east, and how about you, Phil, for the west?"

Gaudy nodded; the responsibility he had awaited had arrived.

"Fine," said Jupiter. "Four or five cars to a section should be enough. Pick your people, assign your territory, and report here at the fire station when you've covered your ground. Look into side roads that are passable but don't go off into the woods as yet. It shouldn't take us an hour if we get started. Any questions?"

There were a number of questions. What should be the boundaries between the sections? How far into the woods roads should they go before giving up? Should the hunt be confined arbitrarily to the township? Jupiter listened, discovered the majority opinion, and announced it as law. In not much more than fifteen minutes cars began pulling out from the curb and the search was on.

During the talk the Maneys had arrived in their truck and, as there were more than enough cars available, he decided to go along with them. He rather favored the idea of patrolling his territory in a deck chair, with his feet on an Oriental rug.

As usual Slim was in cowgirl costume, a scarlet shirt predominating. She looked much too bright-eyed and shining after such a vigorous evening and Jupiter told her so.

"Oh, I went to bed early," she explained. "Those two were up until six."

"If you're so healthy you can drive," Maney said. "Us boys'll sit out in the air."

Jupiter gave her directions and climbed up on the back of the truck. Maney was already seated in one of the two chairs and Joe waved Jupiter to the other. "Take it. I'll be better off lying down. You know it's an odd thing, Boss, but there just happen to be half a dozen bottles of Canadian ale in that icebox."

"Open half of them," Maney ordered, "at once."

As they drove off Jupiter saw Mrs. Fairweather, at the post office door, lift her tiny head in the air before going inside.

"Off we go," Maney said, apparently well pleased with the odd course his morning was taking. He was wearing a black turtle-neck jersey, white flannels, and an expensive Panama hat. "Now then, what do you think has really happened to this fellow?"

Jupiter explained about Howland's appointment with the lady from Boston and his unused bed.

Maney frowned. "Then you think there's a chance he might have met with..."

"Foul play?" Joe said, from the icebox.

"Joe," Maney said, "that stuff is out, as of this moment. Well, if anything has happened to him it would clear up one point for us, eh, Jonesy?"

"I never did think Slim locked you in."

"You didn't? I guess you don't know Slim very well." Joe handed out the opened bottles and settled down on the rug. "Do you think he knows Slim very well, lad?"

Bateman shrugged. "He's a student of human nature. Any fool can see that."

Because of the noise of the truck it was almost necessary to shout. Jupiter said loudly, "There was ugly talk in the post office this morning. They're saying Joe here and Slim are carrying on and might have tried to kill you for the money!"

"Nonsense!" Maney shouted back. "All my money's tied up in my business! I owe everyone! Joe, lad, do you covet my wife?"

Joe nodded. "I certainly do, Boss!"

"I didn't think she was your type."

"They're all my type, love 'em."

"Have you been carrying on with her?"

Joe laughed and winked at Jupiter. "Do I look like the suicidal type?"

Maney roared. "He's right! Just one pass and he'd wake up dead in a ditch!"

Jupiter was not wearing a tie, but, as he recalled last night's embrace in the stable, his neck felt restricted. Of course, he hadn't really made any pass but . . .

The truck suddenly turned off into a cart track and entered the woods.

"Where in hell is this woman taking us?" Joe demanded.

"It's all right," said Maney. "She knows this country like the back of her hand. From riding."

The woods closed in and it was necessary for Maney and Jupiter to get down on the rug with Joe to escape the branches whipping back from the cab of the truck.

"She's doing this because we made her drive," Maney explained happily. "What a girl!"

They lurched along in low gear for half a

mile before rejoining the road they had left. Slim cut the motor and leaned out of the cab. "No sign of him in there!"

"Mighty purty country though, miss," Maney said, getting up. "Drive on."

He slapped at the dirt on his white pants, sat down again in his chair, and took a sip of his ale. "Speaking of women, as we were, gentlemen, how do you account for the fact that they drink more than men?"

"Do they?" Jupiter asked.

"Sure. For every dollar we take in at the bar from a man we get a dollar and a half from a woman. I can show you the figures. Do you suppose women are unhappy or do they just know how to live?"

"A sound drinking man will outdrink a drinking woman, Boss," Joe said.

"I don't deny that. I'm talking about average social drinking. There must be an answer. What is it?"

"They like the taste of it," Joe said. "When I worked in those saloons of yours I'd make up a terrible Martini and a man would gag it down or maybe complain about it. But a woman, she'd sip it like a cat with a dish of cream. Every time. They like the taste of alcohol, it's as simple as that. Don't bother your head with it."

Maney observed Joe thoughtfully for a few seconds and then kicked him sharply in the leg. "That's the stupidest theory I ever heard."

Joe shrugged. "It's a theory. I didn't guarantee how good it was."

"Maybe they're bored, huh?" Maney said, ignoring Joe and looking at Jupiter. "They have time on their hands?"

"Tell him how stupid *that* theory is," said Joe.

While Jupiter was wondering if he was serious, Maney demanded, "Am I right?"

"I think you're generalizing too much about women. You're talking about well-to-do, middle-aged ladies who haven't got much else to occupy them. I doubt if a working girl drinks much more than a working man."

Maney turned to Joe. "You see? Here's a guy who uses his head. He just doesn't come up with some wise-guy answer."

"What's bothering you?" Joe demanded. "Am I supposed to be a college professor this morning?"

"Stuff it," Maney said.

They both tipped up their bottles, angrily. It was impossible for Jupiter to guess whether they were serious or this whole exchange was designed as an elaborate joke on himself.

The truck slowed down and looking ahead he saw a line of parked cars and a crowd gathered in the yard of a house. He thought at first it must have something to do with Howland and then he saw the red flag and the auctioneer standing on a table.

"Stop! Whoa!" Maney yelled when he saw it. He got up and banged on the window of the cab. The truck stopped and Slim climbed out. Maney jumped over the side to the street. "I won't be long."

"What does he want?" Slim asked, and when Joe shrugged, she asked, "Having a nice ride, boys?"

She spread her arms on the side of the truck and rested her chin on her folded hands, smiling at them. Joe said, "Tell her what they're saying in the post office, Jonesy."

When he told her she laughed and reached in and mussed up Bateman's hair. "That'll be the day, huh, Joe?"

"Listen, kid," he said and pushed her hand away from his head, "don't ever touch me. Not even in fun, see?"

"Hey, what is this?" she asked, startled. "What's biting you?"

"How do you think Jack feels about that kind of talk going around? Haven't you got any pride?"

"Pride, shmide," she said disgustedly. "Who cares what they say when a thing isn't true?"

Joe sat shaking his head, then he turned toward her, put one hand on each side of her face, and kissed her. "That's because you're the champion," he said cryptically and sat back again, sighing. "This must be boring for you, Jonesy."

"Not particularly," said Jupiter.

"Jonesy likes to kiss me, too," Slim said. "Don't you, honey?"

"I could learn to love it."

"You'd better not, pal," Joe said and the conversation languished.

It was not a large auction, due perhaps to the counter attraction of the fire horn, but country auctions, Jupiter knew, existed on a hard core of followers, an audience as fanatic and specially informed as balletomanes. In a few minutes Maney was back carrying a Boston rocker of uncertain age and condition.

"Try that, lad," he said and put it on the truck.

Joe sat on it, rocking tentatively. "It's right for size."

"Is it comfortable? Does it relax you to sit in it?"

"It's homey," Joe said. "Thanks, Boss."

"I don't like the idea of a man sitting on the floor." Maney climbed back up on the truck and sat down. "I think we can proceed again, driver."

"Nyaah," said Slim. "I'm tired of steerin' this old thing."

"I'll drive," Jupiter offered and stood up.

There was no objection and he got in front by himself. He felt slightly dazed, less by his hangover and the ale than by the illusive behavior of his passengers. True, they had bad hangovers themselves and there was an unreal quality to the morning itself but he suspected he was witnessing merely a heightened version of their daily routine. It struck him as a rootless routine characterized by enormous, and undirected, vitality. Maney, whose business affairs demanded a measure of thoughtful analysis, must surely have wondered about it. Was the function of Joe, by refusing to be serious, and Slim, by being unequipped for it, to complicate his home life to the point where an examination of his motives was unnecessary? On the other hand Maney and Joe often sat up late at night together and it was possible that they had long, alcoholic discussions resulting in mutual agreement that this was the way to live.

They were on Pleasant Street now, one of the wealthier streets of the town, where an undeclared competition in rural authenticity prevailed. Each farmhouse had been restored to a condition unmatched in its history. Barns were painted, the old stone walls rebuilt, the fields fertilized and lushly green now with new grass. Originally these had been subsistence farms and in a sense they remained so. Although they produced no crops and supported no livestock they provided their owners with the reality of the new American Dream, a sense of security and a place in the country. Not many Americans in their present lifetime would ever live on Pleasant Street but very few Americans had ever attained the old dream of making a million dollars. It was a more sensible dream and, Jupiter supposed, an indication of Progress even though it had come as a result of a violent era and expressed itself most obviously in a concern for the past. The delight in old houses, antiques, square dancing, and the other "simplicities" of country living was merely a surface reaction he believed balanced by a similar enthusiasm for the newest kitchen equipment, jeeps, and modern schools. To Jupiter the handiest symbol of the Dream was the popularity of the deep freeze. Never before in human history had such stocks and varieties of food been so readily available to the consumer and yet the wealthiest householder kept a full freezer in his pantry and his explanation was invariably the same: "I suppose it is foolish but, dammit, I just like the feeling of having it there!" It wasn't food they kept in their freezers, he felt it was fear.

Farther along and more modest than the others was The Wrens' Nest and, seeing Mrs. Wren in her garden, Jupiter turned into the driveway to ask how the doctor was feeling. Mrs. Wren was understandably startled at the contents of the truck but she did her best to cover it up. The doctor, it apeared, was staying in bed this morning on the chance he had caught cold the night before.

"He's really quite all right," she added hastily, apparently feeling that this might be taken as a reflection on Maney as a host. "He's planning to get up for lunch."

"Fine, fine," Maney said. "Give him my regards."

Rocking contentedly in his chair, Joe said,

"You've got a pretty little place here, Mrs. Wren."

"Why, thank you," she said, pleased but still startled.

"All these flowers," Slim observed. "They're cute."

"We're looking for Howland," Jupiter put in and explained the situation.

"My! I'm sure the doctor will be interested to hear what happens."

"It's my hunch, with his wife away, Howie is having a fling at the fleshpots in Boston," Joe said.

"How much more ground have we got to cover, Jonesy?" Maney asked.

"We're about at the end of my section."

"Then let's make a call on the Indian. I took pity on Howland before he left last night and tipped him off about his being around there. I thought it would give him something to work on and it might toss a scare into Arnold."

"You might have mentioned that before," Jupiter said, more sharply than he intended.

"Just remembered it, Cap," Maney said pleasantly.

"Did Howland say he was going to talk to him?"

"He seemed interested in my information but he didn't say what he was going to do about it."

Arnold had not been among those who responded to the fire alarm but that didn't mean anything in itself. "We'd better check," Jupiter said and started the motor.

Arnold lived alone in a shack in the woods two miles away and, although it was well out of the territory Jupiter had assigned himself, he decided it would be simpler to go directly there before reporting back to the others at the fire station. Unlike the night before when he'd had a premonition about the freezer he had no hunch that he'd find anything when he got there. However, when he turned off into the rough logging road that led to the shack he told himself to be ready for anything. And so he was not quite as surprised as he might have been when, coming out into the clearing, he saw Howland's trim, two-toned sedan parked beside Arnold's battered roadster.

He stopped behind them and shut off the motor. The sudden silence was somehow as ominous as the deserted and desolate look of the shack and the clearing. A pair of discarded tires, a rusting engine block, a broken porcelain sink, and other useless items were scattered about the yard. A stovepipe tilted up from the sagging roof of the one-room house and several panes of glass were gone from a window. He got out and slammed the truck door more noisily than was necessary.

Maney, Slim, and Joe were standing up in a line against the cab, looking over its roof toward the shack. For once they appeared relatively subdued.

"We'd better have a look inside, I guess," Jupiter said.

"You look," Joe muttered. "You're the detective."

"I'm game," Maney said and climbed down over the side.

As they were walking across the clearing an ovenbird nearby in the woods shouted, "Teacher, teacher, teacher!" and Jupiter started, he hoped imperceptibly. As a sop to convention he knocked on the door, waited, then lifted the latch and pushed. The door creaked open and there, almost at their feet, his eyes wide in death, was Howland, staring up at them.

8

Once again the ovenbird sounded off and this time Jupiter jumped unabashed. Maney uttered the name of the Saviour, complete with middle initial, and that for the moment seemed to cover the situation. There was no sign of the Indian, inside or out.

Stepping gingerly Jupiter went in and made a hurried, stomach-turning examination of the body. It took no great knowledge of the effect of firearms to ascertain that Howland had died from the charge at close range of a shotgun, through the chest. It was also evident from the abundant dried blood that he had been dead for several hours. It seemed likely that he had been killed inside the shack and that the broken window glass was not the result of Arnold's casual housekeeping but of the blast of the gun. The weapon itself, like the Indian, was not in sight. Maney had remained outside and, in a moment, Jupiter joined him.

"I feel damned near as bad as if I'd killed this poor bastard myself," Maney said quietly.

"I think you'd probably feel a good deal worse," Jupiter said shortly. "There's no reason to blame yourself." He looked out toward the cars and saw that the headlights of Howland's were turned on. That meant...well, the hell with what that meant at the moment. "We'd better get organized. Why don't you and Slim drive back to town and leave Joe here with me for company? You can tell them to alert the state police, the medical examiner, and whatever other public officials this calls for. They've got a real search on their hands now. There's a good chance Arnold is out here in the woods with a shotgun."

"Right," Maney said and Jupiter walked back to the truck with him.

"Another thing," he said to Maney after Slim and Joe had listened to the news, "it might be as well if they got an aggressive character out here to discourage sightseers at the end of the lane."

Joe, informed of his role, climbed into the front of the truck and reappeared with a .22 rifle which had been resting, unknown to Jupiter, behind the seat. "If I'm staying here I'm going to be armed," he announced.

Maney turned the truck around and Slim, unsmiling, waved tentatively at them from the front seat. The lighthearted look of the icebox and chairs out back had disappeared.

Joe was busily loading his gun.

"I trust you're handy with that," Jupiter said.

"I'm lousy. In that last war I was in the Eighth and they stuck me down in the back end of one of those big bombers over Germany. I never touched a feather. And the chances I had!" Finished loading, he brought the gun to his shoulder, aimed, and fired. A bottle at the far edge of the clearing broke into pieces. "I'll be damned! Anyway if the Indian's around he'll know we're here."

"I think I'll have another look inside."

"I'll be outside and if anything happens I'll scream."

Despite the shocking presence of Howland's body Jupiter found himself wondering dispassionately about Arnold and the solitary if not monastic life he led. From the many "art photos" tacked on the walls it was clear that sex was one of his major preoccupations and, while this scarcely set him apart from his fellow man, it was curious that such a remote personality would make such an open display of his interest. Jupiter would have expected to find the pictures tucked away, their fascination enhanced by furtive examination. There was another odder anomaly in evidence; while the yard, the interior of the shack, and Arnold's habitual appearance indicated an almost total disregard for even a minimum of order, Jupiter discovered a thick ledger in which the Indian recorded, in a small, neat hand, his every purchase and payment over a period that must

have extended back for years. There were neither dates nor balances, the incoming and out-
going sums following each other down the
pages as they must have occurred. One random
sequence read:

Bot eats	$7.53
Sold 2 rabbits	50¢
Work 3 days Madison	$17.50
Bot gas	$1.00
Bot 1 gallon wine	$2.40
Sold junk	85¢
Rayked	$3.50
Bot 1 gallon wine	$2.40
Bot woman	$2.00
Axed	$8.00
Bot box shot	$1.59
Bot cigars	35¢
Sold 3 rabbits	75¢

It was a pitifully revealing, purposeless
record, accountable perhaps in terms of a blind
respect for money and yet it must be for Arnold a sort of personal testament of the highest
importance. After each indolent or, of necessity,
strenuous day he was compelled toward his
ledger, to a squaring of accounts with his life,
before he could eat and be lulled by his forti-
fied wine and his rich fantasies of the girls, pro-
vocatively reclining, receptively smiling, and
maddeningly unobtainable on the wall.

The last entry was "Bot 1 qt. whiskey" and it

was easy to imagine him last night loitering half drunk and unwanted on the outskirts of the dance. It was far less easy to imagine him later, shooting down Howland with his rabbit gun. There was no reason to connect him with anyone in the freezer, no motive, except possibly drunken outrage at an intrusion on his privacy, for killing Howland. And yet it was impossible to believe the two incidents were not involved with each other and Arnold with both of them. The most obvious sequence was surely that he had locked the freezer door and killed Howland to escape arrest. But why? Who was his first victim and why?

Arnold's iron cot stood opposite the wall and the door where Howland was lying. Certainly this sheetless bed had never been "made," making it impossible to tell if the Indian had been in it when Howland arrived. Had Howland, leaving the lights on in his car, come to the door, knocked, been invited in, and killed after some talk? Had he walked in believing the Indian was asleep and been shot down without a word? There was no sign of a struggle and certainly Howland would have tried to protect himself if Arnold had picked up his gun and loaded it prior to firing. Could this mean that Arnold was waiting, loaded gun in hand, when Howland drove up? If so, for whom was he waiting? And, again, why?

While absorbed in these questions Jupiter had been absently turning over a pile of pulp magazines obviously selected for their rumpish, bosomy cover illustrations and suddenly he came upon the March issue of the *Moderator*. Since the pulps comprised Arnold's working library it was like finding a parson at a peep show and Jupiter leafed through, stopping at a thumb-grubbed piece called "Buried Treasure" —by Tom Madison.

Although he had read Tom's article before and was familiar, like everyone else in Saxon, with the story of the missing Potter fortune, he sat down on Arnold's bed with the magazine to refresh his memory:

Skeptical folks will tell you old Hiram Potter was a fraud, that he never did have the gold, not $90,000 worth of it anyway. Oh, he might have had some hidden away but if he did it's long since been found and spent. But there are few such skeptics in Saxon, Mass., the town where Hiram lived and died. Most Saxons, young or old, believe in the "Potter Gold" and they've been looking for it off and on for seventy years.

The story goes like this: Potter was a shoemaker by trade and when the sewing machines came out in 1860 he set up a factory—one of the country's first—just in time to turn out boots for the soldiers in the Civil War. They say he made a fortune out of that and it's a matter of record he expanded his factory when the war was over. But then came the famous Black Friday panic in '69 when Jay Gould and Jim Fisk tried to corner the gold market. They say Potter lost heavily and one of the things he lost was his faith in banks. They say he never put another dime in a bank the rest of his days, that he took his profits in gold and hid them so well they've never been found. He was killed in '79 when a runaway horse threw him from his carriage against the stone bridge over the Saxon River and the key to the treasure died with him. It was his widow who set the amount. "Hiram once told me not to worry because he had ninety thousand dollars put away," she is supposed to have said, adding, "but he never did tell me where he'd put it."

She had men in and they went over every inch of the house from cellar to attic; she sent them down the well and she had them dig in a hundred likely places on the property. But not a penny was found. When she passed on five years later her son took over and he tore the house down to its foundations and beyond. Then he, too, went prospecting on Hiram's sixty acres. The family still holds the land, grown up now to birch and pine.

But the skeptics say—and there are men still living who claim to remember him—they say the easy money went to Hiram's head and he became a spender. They tell tales of fast horses and faster women and they say if he told his wife about any hidden money it was to calm her down. They point to these six couplets found scattered through his diary and ask, "Did the man who penned these lines live the life of a hoarder?"

> *To kiss, to hold, I know none finer*
> *Then thee, my love, my fair, Malvina.*
>
> *Abigail, Abigail, of raven tress,*
> *I live but for thy sweet caress.*
>
> *No fire, no flood, no dire calamity,*
> *Could part us now, my darling Amity.*
>
> *Samantha, thou art dear to me.*
> *In truth I hope I am to thee.*
>
> *Fair Patience, spare this yearning heart,*
> *'Twould cease to beat were we to part.*
>
> *Let others travel virtue's path,*
> *Let me know never Virtue's wrath!*

Whatever the truth of the matter may be, small boys—and a few men, too—still defy the stern No Trespassing signs to dig for treasure in the Potter woods. The most persistent and optimistic of these must be Arnold Baxter, a native of the town, who has been at it now for upwards of thirty years. "Oh, the gold is there, all right," he said recently. "That much gold has a kind of smell to it." But wouldn't the gold, if it was found, belong to Hiram's heirs? "Reckon it would, by law," Baxter said and left it at that.

The latest wrinkle has been an attempt to locate the gold by the use of a mine detector but so far...

Jupiter stopped reading and smiled. It was like Tom to dignify Arnold by the use of his full name and that was why he had kept the *Moderator*. How many times had he savored the sight of his name in print? "Arnold Baxter, a native of the town..." He was certainly that.

Jupiter put the magazine back in the shoddy pile and went outside. All right, he told himself grimly, if buried treasure is going to come into this thing, I'm ready for that, too.

Joe was sitting on a stump, his rifle across his knees. "I'm glad I wasn't a Pilgrim, Jonesy. This stuff is rough on the nerves."

Jupiter sat down beside him and they both lit cigarettes. "Did you ever hear of the Potter treasure?"

"Sure. Tommy Madison wrote it up in his tip sheet a while back. What about it?"

Jupiter was a little surprised to learn that Joe read Tom's magazine but then the paraphrase, "In Saxon nearly everyone reads the *Moderator*" came into his mind and he supposed it was true. "You haven't heard any talk about it lately, have you?"

Bateman shook his head. "Weren't there a couple of Joes fooling around there with a mine detector about a year ago?"

"Yes. They didn't have any luck, though."

"Why this interest in gold, Holmes?"

"There has to be a motive for this business. Apparently Arnold's lifework has been looking for the treasure."

"That's right! I remember he said he could smell it. Do you think he's got to it?"

Jupiter looked around the yard and, following his eye, Joe said, "Yeah. I guess not. If Arnold ever hit a jackpot like that he'd clear out of here but fast. Still ..."

"Suppose someone else had struck it and Arnold found out about it. Someone who was in the freezer last night. Do you think Arnold would try to kill four people for a chance at ninety thousand dollars?"

Joe snapped his fingers. "Like that, he would!"

"Would you?"

"That's a nice question." Joe thought about it for a minute. "I'd have to know how good my chances were of getting away with it."

"Four people? Three of them innocent?"

Joe rubbed his hands together and then he laughed. "Hell, no. I've killed enough innocent people."

"I thought you never hit anything."

"I didn't. But I was in the plane, pal, and we weren't carrying mail." He stood up suddenly, aimed at another bottle, and fired. This time he missed. "See? That's me, combat fatigue."

He sat down again and offered Jupiter the gun. "Try your luck?"

"No, thanks. How did you happen to get into bartending?"

"I like to meet interesting people and of course there was that business of eating." He was silent for a time. "If you're leveling I was thinking about college when Jack came up with this other thing. I make jokes for a hundred a week and found, Jonesy. Can Uncle Sam offer me more?"

"How's your future?"

"How's anyone's future? But I can always raise pheasants. You'd be astonished at how much I know about the birds. On the other hand you'd be amazed at how little there is to know about them. I've been meaning to tell you something, Jonesy, and it is this. Don't fool around with Slim."

"Thanks, Joe. As a matter of fact I wasn't planning to."

"She's a nice simple kid but she's acquisitive in a healthy way. She has her eye on you."

"Not on you?"

"Not on me, because I'm smart. You saw how I handled her a while ago. That I-am-dying-for-love-but-I-have-my-code routine. That satisfies her about me. Of course, if either one of us were on a desert isle with her ... but let's not torture ourselves." He sighed. "This Maney is a nice guy but he remains the officer type. Oh, don't apologize, Jonesy, all the Services made their mistakes. Anyway Jack will take very little pushing around and it's not always easy to tell when he considers himself pushed."

"I guess you earn your money."

"Me? Uh, uh. My job is simple. Don't you know what it is?"

"Not exactly."

"I'm here because I think Jack's a bum."

Jupiter laughed. "I might have got that in time."

"Sure. Sure. My God, how he tries to impress me, though! And the hell of it is he's improving. I'm getting to approve of the guy. Still, I'm a long way from losing my job." He dropped his cigarette at his feet and observed it thoughtfully. "Are there any questions?"

"One."

"Let's have it."

"In any of your outings did you do any digging on the Potter place?"

"You're persistent, Jonesy, I'll give you that. No."

"Did you give it any thought?"

"Oh, sure. I remember we kicked it around a couple of nights after we read the magazine, trying to think where the old guy might have tucked it away. But, hell, everybody in town has done that."

"Everybody in town wasn't in that freezer last night. Do you think Maney might have figured an angle and gone after it by himself?"

"I don't think so but he might have. It's the kind of thing he'd get a real bang out of, making me look stupid, aside from the dough... I'm trying to think if we got any ideas... I remember we tried to work out how big a load ninety grand in gold would be. We figured over two hundred pounds but I forget the dimensions." He put his toe on the cigarette and ground it out. "Won't all this get squared away when they catch up with the Indian?"

"It may. But there's a point to be considered. If Arnold locked that door last night there's still someone around he wants to kill. Right now he's loose with a shotgun."

Joe whistled and then there was the sound of a car coming up the lane.

"Here we go," Jupiter said. "Let's not complicate this manhunt by suggesting to anyone there might be two hundred pounds of gold at the end of it. Okay?"

"Check. And, Jonesy, if you need any help on this caper, just remember one thing. I'm yellow."

9

The car, fittingly enough, contained Saxon's three selectmen. Besides Phil Gaudy, there was Fred Talbot, a stout, loquacious chicken breeder, and Herb Cheever, a taciturn, Lincolnesque electrician. The gravity of the occasion sat heavily upon them as they strode silently to the shack, viewed the body, and returned to where Jupiter and Joe had remained standing.

Talbot cleared his throat and said, "A crying shame. A wicked crying shame." Gaudy grunted his agreement and Herb Cheever nodded. "He may ha' been sharp at times but taken all and all Howie was a pretty fair sort of a feller. Most folks liked him, me included." To this the other two agreed also, in their fashion. "Take him callin' a dance, you wouldn't want a man more jovial. Seein' him lyin' dead in there just now ... well, talkin's no use. Don't know what got into Arnold, always been harmless enough, far as I know. What do you make of it, Jones?"

"Arnold must be found, gentlemen," he said quietly. "The quicker the better. He's armed and, I imagine, desperate. I'd like to suggest you put the hunt in the hands of the state police. They're experienced in this kind of thing."

"The state police should be here any minute," Talbot said.

Cheever rocked back on his heels, preparatory to speech. "Town'll want a part in it, Fred."

"Sure, Herb, sure they will," Talbot agreed. "They been looking for Howie, they'll want to go on and look for the Indian."

"This is a bit different," Jupiter said. "I don't think you want to authorize a general disorganized manhunt."

"Well, no, we wouldn't want to do that," Talbot said.

"Coming along up here in the car," Gaudy said, looking at the other two, "we were thinking, with Howie dead, we'd want a man to take his place. Temporarily, that is."

"Of course, when any appointed office is unfilled it falls legally to the Chairman of the Board," Talbot explained. "That'd make Phil, here, Chief of Police."

"I'd be glad enough to take it on," Gaudy said unhappily, "but we were thinking, with things as they are, we'd ask you, seeing as how you've been following the thing and all, to take over for the time being."

Jupiter was not too surprised by the offer. Whenever a difficult or unpleasant job was to be done, in any group of men or women, the person who made the first suggestion usually got elected. "Well, if that's the way you want it."

"You both agree? Phil? Herb?" Talbot asked and when they nodded, "All right then. I guess we can do without any formal swearing in."

Out on the highway a siren wailed, indicating the arrival of Jupiter's new colleagues.

"Congratulations, Chief," Joe said solemnly and shook his hand. "I always wanted to see a guy commissioned in the field."

A local car led the state police and behind them were two other loads of volunteers.

"All right, Bateman," Jupiter said, "get out on the hard road and plug this lane. That's an order."

"Yessir." He started walking, muttering under his breath. "Give a man a little power..."

The two troopers were large, young, and, at the moment, stony-faced. Resolved to play it straight, Jupiter went directly to them and said, "The murdered man is in the house there." They nodded briefly and he tagged along behind them to the shack while they made their inspection.

"Who is he?" one of them asked when they had finished.

"Howland L. Howland. He was Chief of Police."

"Who are you?"

"Edmund Jones, acting Chief of Police."

"You move fast in this town! Whose place is this?"

Jupiter gave them a straightforward account of the case to date, complete with names and thumbnail sketches of the principals involved. He omitted any speculation on the possible motive for it all but by the time he had finished they were reasonably awed. They identified themselves as Officers Kearns and Porter and it appeared that a Detective McCoy, assigned by the District Attorney's office, could be expected within the hour.

"Meanwhile, you got any ideas what we should do, Chief?" Kearns asked. "Will you be setting up a posse to go after this Baxter?"

By now there were at least twenty men in the clearing and, in spite of Joe on the road, more were arriving on foot. They had all known and been friendly with Howland and there was an understandable look of purpose on most of their faces. On the other hand they also knew and had been friendly with Arnold and he doubted if there was any great amount of blood lust among them. Like the selectmen they were stunned and saddened by what had happened but they would be anxious for action. He knew most of them by name and all of them by sight and he didn't like to picture them, haphazardly armed, spreading out nervously into the woods after Arnold. The best thing to do, he supposed, was to select the most level-headed and experienced, split them up into small groups, and give each an area of woods to comb. The others, the willing but unpredictable, he could set to patrolling the roads, harmlessly and in relative safety, in automobiles. He felt suddenly a bit lightheaded and had a wild vision of a bevy of uniformed Boy Scouts beating through the brush with their jackknives. He fought it down, suggested that the troopers stay where they were for the moment, and approached his motley command.

By now most of them were aware of his new status and they gathered slowly to hear his orders. He cleared his throat. "Before we get organized to look for Arnold has anyone any ideas where he might be headed or where he might have holed up?"

There was some murmuring and scratching of heads among them and it gave Jupiter more time to make up his mind which ones to choose for the actual search.

Fred Talbot said, "Clem, here, says he's got a hound can track a man."

Clem Hanford, a large, loose-jointed man, drove a fuel-oil truck for a local company.

"He useter, Fred. I ain't guaranteein' he'll track the Indian. I ain't had him out for two, three years now."

Controlling his enthusiasm for this plan, Jupiter asked, "Is he a bloodhound?"

"Well, he's got some bloodhound in him. I never used him for nawthin' like this though. Just some fun with the boys, now and again."

"I don't see what we can lose by trying him," Jupiter said. "How long would it take you to get him here?"

"He's just over home. I'll git him if you like."

A bloodhound, Jupiter decided, was precisely what they needed and he was surprised he hadn't thought of the idea himself. He was surprised, too, at how simple it was to slip into the pose of authority that pretends to weigh a suggestion before declaring it good.

"Sure. Go get him," he said eagerly.

"Like I say I don't guarantee nawthin'."

"It's worth the try."

When Clem had gone Jupiter quickly selected six men for the official posse. Two were special police officers of the town—the only ones so far on the scene—three were young combat veterans, and the last was the silent selectman, who was also a deer hunter of local renown, Herb Cheever. They departed at once to get firearms, and to the rest, who were showing some signs of chagrin, he announced that he had no objection to any of them arming themselves and remaining on hand in case of need. This satisfied everyone and he returned to the troopers.

"I think it might be a good idea to send out a

description of Baxter. You've got a two-way radio in your car, haven't you?" he asked, and when Kearns nodded he gave them a detailed description of Arnold, ending with, "If you want to know what he really looks like you can turn over a buffalo nickel."

They both grinned at this modest sally and he accompanied them back to their car where he left them and walked over to Howland's sedan with the purpose of turning off its headlights. Arnold's jalopy was parked beside it and he wondered why the Indian hadn't used one of the cars for his getaway. Why had he made no attempt to cover up the crime? It would have been relatively simple for Arnold to have put Howland into the Chief's car, driven it to the other side of town, abandoned it, and returned to his shack through the woods. Or better still he could have buried Howland here in the woods and then got rid of his car. Granted the Indian's reputation for mismanagement it was puzzling he had chosen the worst possible course for his safety.

Jupiter climbed into Howland's car, snapped off the headlights, and sat there looking toward the shack. It seemed clear enough that Howland, informed by Maney that Arnold had been loitering around the basement, had come here last night in the line of duty. But so far this seemed the only clearly motivated action connected with the whole affair. Once, in describing the classic pattern of a murder investigation, Jupiter had employed the analogy of the oceanographer charting the course of a submerged mountain range. A single peak emerging from the calm sea as an island indicated the range and he had likened this to the first act of violence—in this case the locking of the freezer door. Much could be learned from the island itself but the extent and formation of the range could only be determined by repeated soundings. So far his soundings had told him very little and now another island had appeared in the form of Howland's murder. What peaks, lying close to the surface, had he missed between them?

Up to now he had been testing the bottom at random and had learned something about the Maneys, Tom and Mrs. Madison, the Dexters, and Arnold. He had neglected the Wrens because he had felt their murder potential was slight in the extreme. But was it possible to predict anyone's boundary of violence? In the case of the freezer he felt it was possible. Given sufficient motive anyone might kill, but to include three extra uninvolved victims in the killing— as he had indicated earlier to Ginny—demanded something special in the way of rationalization. It demanded that the killer think of the other victims as subhuman, not worthy of life, as the Enemy. Of all the personalities involved only Arnold seemed capable of the act. To him Maney, Dexter, Mrs. Madison, and Dr. Wren might well appear as this enemy

—members of the top level of a society that held him in contempt. Grant him a motive for wanting one of them dead, present him with the sudden, unplanned opportunity of seeing them walk into the freezer, and he might have acted, where in the same situation Slim or Joe, Tom or Ginny, Dot Dexter or Mrs. Wren would have been checked by their identification with the nonvictims.

He was still busy exploring the possibilities of all this when Fred Talbot came up to the car and said, "Clem's back with his hound."

10

The dog was small, elderly, and, for a hound, disturbingly long-haired. Attached to a stout rope he sat at his owner's feet, panting slightly from the exertion of walking up the lane. Sensing that the onlookers were unimpressed with his appearance Clem was defending him. "Like I say he ain't tracked nawthin' for a coupla years and he's gettin' on now. Mebbe his nose is gone for all I know. But he was good once. There's fellers will tell you."

One or two of the men muttered their corroboration of this and Clem said, "Yessir, b'Jesus, he could track a man the same as he could a fox or a coon. Couldn't yer, Ginger?"

Ginger raised a red-rimmed eye at his master and mildly thumped his tail.

"How 'bout deer, Clem?" Cheever asked and, since the hunting of deer with dogs was prohibited by law, there was an exchange of knowing smiles in the crowd.

"Them, too, Herb, if a man had a mind to

put him onto one." He turned to Jupiter. "You want to get something of the Indian's outa the house there?"

"Anything in particular?"

Clem shrugged. "Way he lives most anything oughta stink ample."

This drew some chuckles and, going to the shack, Jupiter sensed that the general mood was changing. Already a few of the men who had gone for weapons were returning and, now that they were armed and the first shock of finding Howland had passed, they were bound to be affected by the "sporting" aspects of the affair. The popularity of hunting was based, he believed, not only on the fact that it released aggressions but that it remained an essentially male activity at a time when male "superiority" was threatened in almost every field. The hard drinking, the obscenity, and the eagerness to "rough" it of the standard hunting party had become a ritual, a hymn to virility.

Jupiter went into the shack, found a pair of stained woolen work pants, and, returning with them, was not surprised to hear a man say, "Let's get after the son-of-a-bitch." It was said less in hatred of Arnold than as a necessary dehumanizing of him as the quarry.

"Just drop them right there," Clem said and led the hound up to the trousers. "There, boy, there! That's what we're after!"

With an expression that combined sadness and boredom Ginger sniffed at the pants. "You fellers stay back now till he picks up a trail—if he does," Clem said. "Find now, boy! Find!"

Clem and the dog began a slow circle at the edge of the clearing around the shack. Most of the men watched in silence as they completed the full circle without success.

"Course this trail must be eight, ten hours old by now," Clem explained, back at the starting point. "I'll try him up close to the house this time."

At the shack Ginger finally showed more interest and then slowly worked his way down to Arnold's car.

"Back trailin'," Cheever said at Jupiter's side. "Start him back at the shack again, Clem!"

"Goin' to!' Clem called.

There was a stir of excitement in the crowd and it was at this moment that Detective McCoy arrived, accompanied by a doctor and another pair of troopers. There was a brief conference between the new arrivals and Officers Kearns and Porter and then the whole group moved toward the shack.

"Keep back, Goddamit!" Clem shouted to them. "Can't yer see what we're doin' here?"

McCoy, a husky, silver-haired man in a gabardine suit, hesitated and Jupiter walked over to him. Officer Kearns muttered an introduction and the detective said, "Glad to know you, Chief. Going to let us see the body?"

"Happy to have you," Jupiter said. "Want to

go right in now or wait and see if the hound picks up a trail?"

Unhappily Ginger chose this instant to sit down and scratch his ear. McCoy looked at the dog without enthusiasm and moved a wooden match from one side of his mouth to the other. "How long has the nigger been missing?"

Jupiter was not eager to quarrel with McCoy but so far it had been a morning of stands and he decided to continue on that basis. "The man we're looking for is not a Negro. He's part Indian and he must have been gone under ten hours."

McCoy tipped his head to one side and smiled, shifting the match again in his mouth. "Ten hours is a big start. A man can go a long way in that time."

"If he keeps going, yes."

Once more Ginger began to work slowly down from the shack to the parked cars but he lost the scent there and, after sniffing futilely for a time, sat down and scratched again. Clem pulled him up sharply and led him back to the shack.

"Come on, Doc," McCoy said and the official party moved along to the house.

A man came up and muttered something disrespectful about "them staters" but Jupiter was not annoyed. It had been his desire from the start that the state police handle the search for Arnold while he concentrated on the more interesting problem of the freezer.

Clem let Ginger circle the house three more times, then walked back to Jupiter.

"No luck?"

"Looks to me like he musta run off down the lane here to the hard road," Clem said. "Trouble is the lane's all trampled to hell and gone by the fellers walkin' up and down it."

"Do you think he was on him there for a while?"

"Wouldn't care to say for sure. Scent don't hang good on open ground like this with the sun on it."

"Do you think it's possible he might pick up the scent after all this time?"

"Time don't matter so much as conditions. Take in the woods when the leaves and grass is damp, scent'll hold one hell of a long time. I read of hounds followin' a track forty-eight hours old. Ginger, here, never done nawthin' like that, though."

"Why don't you try a bigger circle deeper in the woods?"

"Goin' to," Clem said and set off. "Give yer a yell if he comes on to anythin'."

Jupiter looked at his watch, saw it was past midday, and wandered up to the shack where Kearns and Porter were relating to McCoy the information he had given them earlier. The doctor remained inside.

"Maney," McCoy said. "Is that Jack Maney who owns the taverns?"

Jupiter nodded. "Do you know him?"

"I'm met him. Well. Are you a friend of Mr. Maney's, Mr. Jones?"

"I'm a neighbor anyway. I was with him when we found Howland."

McCoy removed the match from his mouth and smiled at Jupiter and this time his smile was much warmer. "We'll want to co-operate all we can on this with you, Mr. Jones."

"That's fine," said Jupiter, keeping his face straight. "We'll do all we can to co-operate, Mr. McCoy."

"Michael J. McCoy. Mike," McCoy said and put out his hand.

"Edmund Jones. Ed," Jupiter said and shook the hand.

"Where's Maney now, Ed?"

"I don't know, Mike. He went back to town to spread the alarm and he may have taken his wife home. She was with us."

"Uh, huh. The reason I ask is on account of the papers. This killing has to tie in with the whing-ding at Maney's last night, the way you look at it?"

"I believe so, yes. There's no evidence."

"No evidence. Well. How would this be? The guy is a nut. He locks them in, he's seen around, and Howland is killed coming out here to pick him up?"

"Crazed Indian sought in Saxon killing?"

McCoy brightened. "Yeah! What do you think of it?"

"For the papers or for what actually happened?"

"We'll find out what happened when we get the bastard," McCoy said shortly. "And about that, Ed. Let's keep the citizens out of the woods, huh? You send those boys creeping through thickets after this Indian and sure as you're born they'll start whapping at each other. They'll get jumpy."

Although he privately agreed about this Jupiter felt obligated to say, "They look sound enough to me."

"Now they do. But give them two hours out there thinking about him popping out from the next tree and they'll look different to you. You been in police work very long, Ed?"

"Pretty long. About half an hour."

McCoy laughed and slapped him on the shoulder. "Swell! Swell! Well, look, boy, the way we handle a thing like this, a guy busts out of the pen or takes off like this joker, we just let him sit, see? We can't cover the whole county. Sooner or later he gets hungry and he'll show. We watch spots, sure, and we send out his description, all that. When he shows we'll go after him. We've even got bloodhounds, real ones. But this trail is cold. Ten hours! He could be in New York City!"

"If he was headed for New York why did he leave two automobiles?"

McCoy hunched his shoulders. "All right. You want bloodhounds, Ed, I'll get bloodhounds. But will you keep the citizens out of the woods?"

"Sure. As a matter of fact, I'm not certain Arnold wouldn't think of bloodhounds himself. He could easily have taken a walk in the Saxon River."

"There you are! I'll lay you a bet we pick this guy up in two days. Three at the outside."

Jupiter shook his head. "In that case I don't like your newspaper story. Have you got any idea how people are going to feel in this town when they read a homicidal maniac is loose? We have people without phones, people living on back roads, women living alone, we can't..."

"What are you going to tell them?"

"What's wrong with the truth? We don't believe he's a maniac, and we're investigating his motive for locking the freezer door and killing Howland?"

McCoy sucked his lip. "I don't like that much. It points straight to Maney."

"Why?"

"Who were the other people in there? A retired dentist, a society woman, a guy who makes signs in his home workshop? It happened at Maney's and people are going to put two and two together. They'll figure Maney was the victim."

"Well, what's wrong with that?"

"What's wrong with that? Maney doesn't think he was the victim, does he?"

"No. As far as I know none of them do."

"I don't care about the others so much. It's Maney I'm worried about. I give out a line he's tied up in it and..." McCoy drew his forefinger across his throat. "That's what happens to me."

"Could Maney do that?"

"Maney could do that," he said definitely. "I don't know as I'd blame him so much, either. Murder's a touchy business. Innocent people don't like to get fouled up in it. Not in the papers, anyway. This looks like a crackpot job to me as it stands now and that's the story I'm giving out. But I'll tell you what I'll do for you. In a couple of hours we'll report the Indian was seen in Boston. That'll calm your natives."

Jupiter examined the ethics of this proposition and found them wanting. "Suppose I give out my own story and then we'll both be covered."

"If you want it that way." McCoy lit a cigarette with some care. "I'd like it if we could work together on the thing, Ed."

"I think we can. But Arnold's no homicidal maniac. A man can go crazy but it would be too much of a coincidence for him to go crazy at the precise moment those four people walked into the freezer. He had to have something against one of them."

"Maybe. Maybe not. People do things you can't explain at all. A guy living the way he does is crazy to start with in my book. He can go for a long time and never get into trouble and then..." He snapped his fingers. "Just like that.

Well, I'll finish up here and get over and talk to Maney. He may see it your way."

Clem and Ginger had given up. With their failure much of the urgency had gone out of the hunting party. But enough remained so that there was some grumbling when Jupiter announced McCoy's plan to sit tight and wait for Arnold to make a break. It was Herb Cheever, the deer hunter, who put an end to most of it. "Feller's right," he said. "You'll never catch up with Arnold in the woods without a dog, trailin' him. This season o' the year, with the leaves on, you could walk right by him. Arnold knows that same as me. But he ain't too smart. He'll show himself and that's when we can go after him."

It was decided to hold Ginger in readiness with a small force at the fire station. One long blast on the horn would be the signal Arnold had been sighted. It was agreed, too, that night would be the most dangerous time and a check-up should be made to assure the presence of an armed male in every household in town. Not a few jokes were offered on the subject of who should get what elderly spinster or widow and a general meeting was called for seven o'clock at the fire station to discuss it.

Like a snowstorm or a heat wave the affair would draw the town together in an awareness of a common dilemma. I must do some thinking, Jupiter decided, on the holiday spirit of crises.

He had noticed Harry Dexter, unarmed,

among the late arrivals in the clearing and now Dexter came up to him.

"This is a terrible thing," said the blacksmith, clearly upset.

Jupiter agreed that it was.

"Poor Arnold," Harry said.

"Poor Howland."

"Well, yes, of course. It's hard to think of Arnold as a killer, though. Was it he who locked the door on us last night, do you think?"

"It looks that way, Harry."

"Then I'm responsible for the whole damned thing," Dexter said, unhappily. "He was trying to kill me!"

11

Jupiter said, "Hold it, Harry. Detective McCoy should hear this if you're serious."

"I'm serious enough."

"Come on then." He led Dexter to the shack and introduced him to McCoy. Harry didn't look in at the body.

"Arnold and I had a fight yesterday morning," Dexter began. "We've been having cesspool trouble at our house and I asked Arnold if he'd dig a ditch for me so I could lay an overflow pipe. He came Tuesday as he'd promised, and got it about half dug but he didn't show up the next day. I saw him that afternoon in town and, well, he had an excuse. I think he said he'd had to cut the lawn in the cemetery because there was going to be a funeral. You know Arnold, Jones."

"Uh, huh," said Jupiter.

"I wasn't too mad at him then because he's done work for me off and on and always before he's finished a job if he said he'd take it on in the first place. I asked him if he'd be there Thursday and he said he would. But again he didn't show up and Friday, yesterday morning, I saw him in the village hanging around doing nothing. I asked him what the trouble was and he said he guessed he didn't feel like working. Not even an excuse this time." Harry licked his lips. "Well, we had words. I was mad. He made a couple of remarks about Dorothy and I ended up by calling him a no-good, half-breed bum."

Apparently this was the end of the story. Dexter, looking very uncomfortable, stared at the ground. McCoy raised his eyebrows at Jupiter. "You call that a motive for murder, Mr. Dexter?"

"It was a terrible thing to call a man," Harry said. "I don't understand how I could have done it."

Dexter was still looking at the ground and McCoy, catching Jupiter's eye, made a circle with his forefinger at the side of his head.

Jupiter said, "I'd guess Arnold has been called worse than that before, Harry. I know how you probably feel but do you really think he'd try to kill you because of it?"

"What other reason would he have?" Harry asked. "He must have been hanging around there last night surly drunk and when he saw us walk into the freezer he decided to get back at me. Don't you see? I've been one of the few people in town who ever treated him like a human being and I'd turned on him like that."

McCoy coughed. "I wouldn't worry about it if I were you, Mr. Dexter. It seems to me you had a pretty good reason to call him a bum. The more I hear about him the more I'm convinced he's crazy."

"It wasn't calling him a bum that matters. I called him . . ."

"Harry," Jupiter said. "My car's back in the village. There's nothing more to do around here and I'd like to get home for some lunch. Would you give me a lift?" Harry nodded doubtfully and Jupiter turned to McCoy. "I'll keep in touch with you, Mike."

Most of the men were leaving the clearing and Jupiter and Dexter walked out the lane with them, not speaking. Joe Bateman was still on duty, holding in check a sizable gathering of men, women, and children.

"Any orders, Chief?" he asked.

Jupiter explained that McCoy would be out shortly on his way to Maney's and suggested he go along to show him the way. "He'll probably want to put one of his men on here anyway."

"Right, Chief," Joe said and saluted snappily.

They went along to Dexter's jeep but before starting the motor Harry said, "I've just been thinking how all that must have sounded. Lord! It doesn't make much sense, does it?"

"Not to McCoy. But there's a chance it did have something to do with it. It's too bad you didn't mention it last night."

"But I didn't even know Arnold was there

124

last night! It was only, just now, when I heard about Howland being dead out here in Arnold's shack..." He brushed one hand across his forehead and started the motor. "Has anyone else had a fight with Arnold? Maney or Dr. Wren or Mrs. Madison?"

"That's the point, Harry, none of them has as far as I know. That's why there may be something to this business of yours. But McCoy's right on one thing. If Arnold did lock you in he was out of his head. There's no reason to blame yourself."

"I'm afraid I can't agree on that." Dexter drove sitting up straight, his arms stiff on the wheel. "If I precipitated this by calling him a half-breed then a measure of guilt belongs to me. It was an unforgivable thing to do anyway and I was going to apologize to him today."

Jupiter twisted his long legs into some semblance of comfort and sighed. "This is a difficult moment in history to live like a gentleman, Harry."

"That may be, but a man can try."

"I think it's possible to be an old gentleman or a young gentleman but you're going to knock yourself out trying to be a middle-aged gentleman." He paused and then went on thoughtfully. "I don't know all your reasons for moving to the country, but I'd guess they were fairly standard. You wanted to get away from the compromises of big city business life, wasn't that it?"

"Partly. Mostly, perhaps."

"There're lots of ways to do it. Write a book, join the church, join the Communist Party, commit suicide, or buy a blacksmith shop in the country. You picked the toughest. There's no honey in it for a middle-aged man. We're still victims of our upbringing and we expect ourselves to do a man's job. You're not doing a man's job."

"The hell I'm not!" Harry flared.

"You're a professional hobbyist, a crafter, selling your stuff in Gift Shoppes."

"By God, Jones, I'll..."

"Sure. Go ahead. Call me a half-breed."

Dexter had not been driving fast but now he slowed his jeep to a crawl. "I deserve this," he said quietly. "Go on."

"It's an odd thing to question a blacksmith's virility but that's what you've been doing to yourself. That's why an old man can be a gentleman; he's through worrying about his virility and a young man doesn't question it. You're unconsciously ashamed of your work and you ought to be back in New York cheating people."

"There's probably some truth in that," Dexter admitted after a moment. "Yes, I think there is, as much as I dislike amateur psychiatry."

"I apologize for that but it's standard equipment for detectives these days and I'm the Chief of Police."

Harry's eyes were partly closed. "I'd never have lost my head as I did with Arnold back in

New York. I had greater provocation than that but I never hit below the belt."

"How were you in New York on the question of falling in love with other men's wives?"

This time Dexter brought the car to a complete stop at the side of the road. "I consider that question way below the belt."

"So do I but I'm not being a gentleman now, Harry, I'm being a policeman."

"What possible connection could all this have with Arnold?"

Jupiter shrugged. "I don't know. It has to do with you and Maney, two of the people who were in that freezer."

"Very well. What do you want to know?"

"Does Maney know you've asked Slim to marry you?"

Harry sucked in his breath sharply. "I'd certainly like to know how you found that out."

"She told me." Dexter's face was white and Jupiter, conscious that he must be suffering, said, "A man has been killed and tonight plenty of people here in town are going to be honestly frightened Arnold might pop in on them. If I can find out anything that will get this thing over any sooner I'm going to do it. You're getting the shock treatment because you happen to be a guy I think it'll work on. Slim didn't say if Jack knew anything about you and I want to know if you, with your strict code of honor, went to him with your intentions."

Harry put both hands to his head and rubbed

his temple. "No. No, I haven't said anything to him." He dropped his hands and faced Jupiter. "This can't have anything to do with Arnold, damn you! Aren't you just working out a few aggressions of your own?"

"Quite possibly, but listen to this. Suppose Maney did know about it, got jealous, and decided to kill you?"

"That's impossible, he was in . . ."

"That's right. He was in there with you. But suppose he had Joe Bateman lock the door in order to build up an alibi for himself later? If you were found dead in a couple of days Maney wouldn't be suspected."

"That's fantastic! Joe wouldn't be a party to . . ."

"Suppose Arnold saw Bateman lock the door and hung around last night to try and blackmail him. Suppose Maney and Bateman scared him off and Arnold went home. A car drives in and he loads his gun, thinking it was Maney. Howland gets killed instead." Jupiter stopped and swallowed. It was an improvisation but it sobered him. Suppose something like that *had* happened? "I'll admit it's fantastic but I have to work on possibilities. It's not a great deal more fantastic than the idea Arnold tired to kill you and three people just because you called him a nasty name."

Dexter put the car in gear and once again they headed slowly toward the village. Looking straight ahead Harry asked quietly, "What did Slim have to say about me?"

Jupiter sighed. "She thinks you're sweet."

"As bad as that, huh?"

"I'm afraid so. Can you stand any more amateur psychiatry? I'd like to give you the famous Jones sixty-second analysis."

Dexter was able to smile. "All right."

"You unerringly picked a woman to fall in love with whom you couldn't possibly get, because you wanted to tantalize yourself with the chase. We call that a sign of adolescence but you can call it love if you want to."

"I can't get her out of my mind. I've tried but..."

"The only way you'll get her out of your mind is to become really popular with yourself. Treatment: repeat to yourself twice daily that you had guts enough to get out of New York, and guts enough to make pretty little signs for a living, and guts enough to try and be a middle-aged gentleman. Do that and adopt two or three small children and you're cured." He observed Dexter's surprise with amusement. "That was less than sixty seconds. There'll be no charge."

They were in the village and Harry drew up to the curb and cut the motor. "You're a glib son-of-a-gun, Jones, and I don't think I like you but I suppose there is some sense in what you say. We've thought of adopting children but..."

"But what?"

"It's a question of money mostly. We don't live on what I earn even now."

"It's my theory the simple life is not for everyone. You have to be either very rich or very poor, very talented or very dull. Happily for me I'm both rich and talented." He climbed over the door of the jeep. "Get yourself those kids, Harry, they'll keep you poor."

He walked into the liquor store without looking back. Harry had been dead right—he was working off a large accumulation of aggressions this morning.

Vito Polletti, the small, alert proprietor of the liquor store, bowed deeply. It was apparent that, in spite of the circumstances, he was prepared to carry through their familiar private ritual. Jupiter bowed back without speaking, walked over to the whiskey shelves, and pretended to examine their contents.

"My God!" he said finally. "What prices! You're a robber, Polletti!"

Vito waved his arms. "Taxis! Thassa all she is, Boss, taxis!"

"Goddam government!"

"Goddam everytin'!"

The ritual complete, Jupiter pulled a chair out from the wall and sat down. "All right, Vito, where's Arnold?"

Vito cocked his head and smiled. "I hafta laugh. Ha. Ha. They maka you Chiefa da Police. Ha. Ha."

"Ha. Ha. Where's Arnold?"

"I show you, justa minute." He went behind the counter and brought out a large hand-drawn map mounted on cardboard. It was a map of Saxon he had made himself to direct strangers around the town. His was the only store open after six o'clock at night and his map saw a good deal of service. He put the board on Jupiter's lap and pointed with a pencil. "Thissa here where da Innian live. He go downa road here, turna here, come to da rive, walka da rive, stoppa here. Thissa beeg swumpy place he catcha muskrattas in winner. Beega place, two, t'ree mile. Swumpy."

"I know. I walked into it once."

"You go fin' him in thissa place?"

"What do you think?"

"I tell you what I think." He put his pencil away, went to the middle of the store and crouched down, his hands out as if he were holding a gun. "Here'sa you, some udder fella, walkin' in da swump." He lifted his legs high and pretended to stagger. "Makea helluva noise. Innian lissen." Here Vito cupped his ear, one finger in the air. "You come too close. Booma! You dead Chiefa da Police!"

Jupiter sighed. "So much for that plan. Now what do you suggest?"

Vito brought out his pencil again, studied the map and drew in a tiny square at the far end of the swamp, a short distance in from a back road.

"Nicea colored lady live here. Ver' nice. She's

131

a good fren' da Innian. Some time, tonight, nex' day, he go see her. He trust her."

"I see," Jupiter said finally.

Vito was watching him closely. "You likea da job, Chiefa da Police?"

"He killed Howland."

"Thassa right, Boss." Vito cocked his head again, grinning. "You one helluva Chiefa da Police. Tough guy."

"You're an anarchist, Polletti. I may take my trade elsewhere. Do you happen to know where all these taxes go? They support the state police and there's a Detective McCoy in town. He shall hear about this colored lady and deal with the situation properly."

Vito shook his head, still grinning. "Chiefa da Police. Ha. Ha. Beega shot."

"I can be provoked, you know. I could haul you in right now for withholding important information."

"Wassa that?"

"One bottle of whiskey."

Vito frowned. "I don' getcha, Boss."

"Yesterday or the day before Arnold bought a bottle of whiskey in here. You should have told me about it."

"Thassa not right! No!" He shook his head vigorously and pointed to a row of gallon bottles of wine on the floor. "Thassa what he drink. All time."

"All except the bottle of whiskey."

Vito ran to the back of the store, opened a

door, and called something in rapid Italian. Mrs. Polletti answered him at length but apparently in the negative. He returned and hunched his shoulders. "Not in here, Boss."

"That's very interesting." He got up and went to the door, where he stopped and pointed at his chest. "Chiefa da Police! Smart guy!"

12

"Where was the fire?"

The children were having lunch and it was Betty who asked the question. For an instant he couldn't think what she meant and then he said casually, "False alarm. Did you have a busy morning, dear?"

She seemed mildly suspicious but she said, "It was such a beautiful day to be outdoors I hurried through the breakfast dishes, changed the beds, sorted the laundry, vacuumed downstairs, washed the kitchen floor, waxed it, hung up the bedroom curtains I'd ironed yesterday, picked up Ricky's clothes after he emptied his bureau, washed the bathroom wall where Mark painted with the shoe polish, sewed up Susan's doll's dress where it was ripped, and got out to feed the chickens and collect the eggs just before you got home."

"Fine," Jupiter said. "How many eggs did we get?"

"Seven, so far."

"Eight," Susan said. "Mark broke one."

"Ri'hy pooed me," Mark explained.

"That's okay," Jupiter said. "Those things happen. Eat your lunch."

"And you?" Betty asked. "What of your morning?"

He stretched out on the kitchen couch and sighed. "I think I made a bad mistake going out at all this morning. I ticked off Mrs. Fairweather at the post office for gossiping and one thing led to another."

Betty said, "Ginny Garrett called up about half an hour ago. If she wasn't such a sane, level-headed girl I wouldn't..."

"Oh," Jupiter said. "Then you know I've had a trying morning. How about something to eat?"

"Peanut butter sandwich, Chief?"

"Yes. I have a clue I'd like you to examine. Arnold is a wine drinker and he has always bought it from Vito but recently he seems to have bought a bottle of whiskey and not from Vito. What does that suggest to you?" He lit a cigarette and did not wait for her answer. "To me it suggests that he has hit a sizable and illegal source of income. What would that be?"

"Blackmail?"

"Possibly. But if he was blackmailing one of the people in the freezer it would be folly for him to try and kill him."

"Maybe he stole something and was threatened with exposure."

135

"That's quick thinking but a little too quick. A simple robbery would have been reported by now. There would be nothing to hide. Unless ...unless the owner of the stolen property had something to hide, something to do with the property itself." She brought him his sandwich and a glass of milk. "Thank you. I don't like to cause you any alarm but I think there's a good chance the Potter treasure has been found."

"Are you really serious?"

"It would fit and something has to fit. I don't believe for a minute Arnold is insane. I saw him last night and he certainly had his wits about him then. He claimed all he was doing in the basement was trying to steal a couple of pheasants and Maney and I let him go. It was a mistake that cost Howland his life."

"While we're on the subject," Betty said, "I hope you're not going to let this Chief of Police business go to your head. Don't get too brave now."

He munched his sandwich. "You can count on me. As a matter of fact Vito believes Arnold has holed up in that big swamp on the other side of town and I'm turning that part of the business over to my good friend Mike McCoy, State Detective."

"Of that I approve."

"This thing is not without fascination, though. Suppose Wren, Maney, Harry, or, conceivably, Mrs. Madison has located the gold? What a thing! No, wait a minute. Maybe Arnold found it—he's been looking for it long enough —he found it and one of them knows he did. He knew they knew and . . . The hell with it, I'm confusing myself."

"Can't you wait until Arnold is arrested?"

"Me? Wait? I dig, probe, figure angles. Slowly the hidden truth begins to take shape in my mind. I'm grim, tenacious, a bulldog, I mean a bloodhound, on the trail. Did Ginny tell you about the bloodhound?"

"She mentioned there was one."

"I don't see why I shouldn't have a bloodhound of my own. We ought to have a dog on the place."

"My! You're certainly wound up." She smiled at him. "It's like old times. I think it's good for you."

"Oddly, except for the bloodshed involved, this may have a salutary effect on a number of people in town. A catalytic agent, like a war. It may cure Harry for one thing. If there's anything I can't stand in the country it's a neurotic blacksmith. I'm working on the Dexters to adopt some children."

"According to Ginny you did some work on Tom."

"How's that?"

"He's decided to give up the *Moderator*."

"I'm not sure that's a good idea. I'll have to talk to him about it. I'm going to have a little talk with Mrs. Madison too. It's high time Ginny

137

and Tom were married. Oh, by the way. Joe Bateman tells me Slim has her eye on me."

"Oh, she has, has she? I think I'd better get a sitter and go along with you this afternoon."

"You can try, but I doubt if you'll be able to get one. Who'd stay alone way out here knowing Arnold was loose? No. I'll load the twelve-gauge for you and you can sit out on the back step with it across your knees."

"That would be one way to amuse the children, certainly."

She looked just a bit uncomfortable and he said, "Actually there's little chance Arnold will appear in daylight. Would you like me to get somebody to stay with you?"

"It's not that. I just don't like to miss all the excitement."

"If there's any excitement I'll come back for you. There's been a lot of ugly talk about my not taking an interest in the town affairs, otherwise I'd stay home myself."

"Uh, huh."

He turned on the radio for the hourly news and one of the first bulletins announced:

Chief of Police Howland L. Howland of Saxon was found shot to death this morning in a lonely shack in the woods of that town. A statewide search is under way for Arnold Baxter, owner of the shack, who, police believe, is responsible for the slaying. No motive is known for the killing

138

and police fear Baxter, an Indian, may have become mentally deranged following an argument with the policeman.

In Washington today...

Jupiter snapped off the radio angrily. "If that's what McCoy calls co-operation! Well, it's time I got back to the old drawing board. I'm going to call on the Wrens. I've neglected them but I've had my eye on them right along. Much too innocent-looking. Hold the fort, dear!"

13

When Jupiter drove in, Mrs. Wren was still at work in her garden while the doctor was up, dressed, and, as he described it, "Just puttering about the place."

"Yes, my boy," he said after they had exchanged the proper sentiments about Howland's death and Arnold's disappearance, "just puttering about the place. Plenty to be done but I can't seem to settle down to anything. It's a shocking affair. Shocking."

"You can't think of any reason why Arnold might have locked you all in, I suppose?"

"Not the slightest. Why, I didn't know until just now that Arnold was around there last night."

"No, John," Mrs. Wren said. "Don't you remember we saw him as we were leaving last night? When we were in the car?"

"Did we, my dear? I'm afraid I didn't...Did you speak of seeing him?"

Mrs. Wren was suddenly embarrassed.

"When I turned on the lights of the car he was standing there. I suppose you don't remember." She looked at Jupiter and sighed. "I'm afraid he was..."

"We have no secrets from Mr. Jones on that score, my dear. He could see for himself that I was plastered."

"John! You were nothing of the sort."

Wren winked at Jupiter. "Be that as it may. At any rate, I don't seem to recall seeing Arnold, the Indian, or any other Indian. I suppose he'll be caught sooner or later."

"The state police are working on it," Jupiter said.

"It's frightening to think of him just...loose in the woods," Mrs. Wren said and shuddered slightly.

"That's the reason I dropped in," Jupiter said. "I don't think there's too much chance of his coming here but I wonder if you want me to arrange for someone to stay with you tonight. After all you were one of the people in the freezer, Doctor."

"That's very kind of you," Wren said. "But I really don't think—" He paused when his wife started to protest. "I do think I can protect myself, my dear. I have a pistol."

"But, John, we both sleep like logs. Anyone could walk in and we'd never wake up! Don't you remember the time that dog..."

"Well, frankly, if Arnold should break in he'd be welcome to anything in the house. Food or money, that is. I'm sure he wouldn't want to kill us in our beds. But if you'd feel safer, my dear..."

"I do think I would."

"All right then," Jupiter said. "I'll have someone here before dark."

"Thank you, Mr. Jones," said Wren. "It's a little early in the day but before you leave would you care for—"

"John."

Wren turned to her, a faint flush coming into his cheeks. "I'm sixty-five years old, Emily, and capable of deciding when I do or do not want to take a drink. Furthermore—"

Jupiter said hastily, "I honestly don't feel too much—"

"Furthermore, it so happens Mr. Jones saved my life last night and neither of us has so much as mentioned our thanks to him." He turned to Jupiter. "It would be a pleasure and an honor to have a drink with you, sir."

"Of course. Please do, Mr. Jones," said Mrs. Wren, quickly.

Deciding that Wren would have the drink whether he joined him or not, Jupiter said, "If you put it that way, Doctor, I don't see how I can refuse."

Mrs. Wren returned to her gardening and, after sniffing at her retreating back, the doctor led Jupiter into the kitchen. The Wrens' Nest differed from most old Cape Cod houses in that no wing had ever been added at the rear of this one and the original low-ceilinged kitchen, as the Wrens proudly pointed out to all visitors, remained intact. Wren was a fairly tall man and Jupiter sat down and watched with some fascination as his host got out the bottle and glasses; he seemed to employ a kind of batlike radar system, ducking at the last instant under the ancient beams.

"Don't you ever hit your head?" Jupiter asked finally.

"Frequently," Wren answered, smiling. "Hardly a night passes without my striking myself on the damned things. Of course, by the time it happens I've usually built up quite a high immunity to pain. Still, I will say it's an inconvenience. Straight or with water?"

"With water, please."

"Yes, it's a price to pay for individuality. The house was built in 1740, you know, the oldest in town. That has meaning for me, Jones, despite the blows on the head. Living up to an old place like this does dominate our lives, I suppose, but I don't think I could ever be happy in the standard horrors they are putting up today."

Jupiter reflected that in 1740 the Cape Cod was as rigidly standard a design as that used in the most unimaginative housing development of today but he made no comment on this. As Wren passed him his drink he had a sudden inspiration.

Jupiter lifted his glass and, as the doctor

143

started to drink said, quietly but clearly, "To the Potter treasure."

He had decided it would be an excellent if a bit unsporting test and had set himself to watch Wren for the slightest tremor of reaction. But the reaction was sudden, violent, and alarming; Wren choked on the drink, spilled what was left in his glass, and doubled over gasping for breath. Jupiter got up quickly, struck his head sharply on a beam, and went to his side. He slapped the doctor on the back with one hand and massaged his own head with the other. Wren sank into a chair, his eyes streaming, while Jupiter, stooping carefully, went to the sink for a glass of water.

It was at least three minutes before Wren could speak. Finally he wiped his eyes, took a sip of water, and said, "Down the windpipe... painful... very painful."

Jupiter, deciding to wait him out, said nothing.

The doctor, shaking his head, said, "I must apologize... yes. Took me by surprise with that toast... How did you know?"

"Maybe you'd better tell me about it, Dr. Wren," Jupiter said firmly. It was, to him, a fairly tense moment.

Wren seemed quite startled with this suggestion. "Why... why, what do you mean? I have the Potters' permission to hunt for the gold but I've never told anyone else, except Emily, that

I'm looking for it. Did you see me on the Potter place? Is that how you knew?"

"No. I didn't see you there, Doctor."

"You didn't? Well, it's astonishing to me how you could have known what I was up to. Of course, I hope you'll keep it a secret between us because, well, you know it is rather a...boyish enterprise." He got up and poured himself a new drink. "The thing has always fascinated me and when Tom's article came out I said to myself, well, I'll have a shot at it myself." He raised his glass. "As you say, to the Potter treasure."

Jupiter let him drink his fill this time without interruption before he said, "Then you don't know the gold has been discovered?"

Wren set his glass down with a bang. "No! Where?"

"I can't tell you right now," Jupiter said, which was true enough.

"But who...do you mean its discovery has something to do with Howland and Arnold?"

"Yes. Didn't you know Arnold has been after it for a long time?"

Wren frowned. "Yes, of course. Tom mentioned that in his article."

"You never saw Arnold when you were searching the Potter land?"

"No. Actually I haven't done a great deal of searching. Here, let me show you." He got up, went into the living room, and returned with a large loose-leaf notebook. He stood with it in his hands. "I can't seem to realize the treasure has been found. Who discovered it? Has it been turned over to the Potter estate?"

"I can't answer those questions right now, Doctor. When we catch up with Arnold I'm sure the true story will come out."

"It's incredible! Really, it is! To think that after all these years...well, I don't suppose you'll be interested in my researches."

"I'd like to see what you've done. It might be some help in the investigation," Jupiter said.

"But I really don't understand. If the treasure has been unearthed...if you know who has found it..."

"Well, I really don't know who has found it and I don't know where it was found but I'm convinced Arnold is in on it. It's my guess he also locked the freezer door trying to kill the other person involved. You see..."

"But my heavens! When I choked just now you must have thought I was that person!"

"I'll admit the thought did enter my head."

"Of course! Why, you were trying to trick me!" He seemed quite pleased with this thought and then he frowned. "Do you really think it's one of the others? Maney or Dexter or Mrs. Madison?"

"It looks that way, yes. You haven't noticed any one of them on the Potter place, have you?"

"No, I never have...that is..."

"Yes?"

"I should hate to involve anyone unnecessarily, you know. Well, that is, I have seen Mrs.

Maney riding through there once or twice. On horseback, you know."

"Did you speak to her?"

"Oh, no, no. She didn't see me at all. That is, I hid myself. I've taken some pains no one should discover my silly pastime. That's what I feel it is, you know. What I have felt, I should say. I'm going to miss it." He opened the notebook and withdrew a separate sheet of paper. "Here is my authorization from the Potter estate to look for the money. And I also have a contract with them for 25 per cent of anything I might turn up."

"Twenty-five per cent? That doesn't seem too generous."

"Well, no, perhaps not. But they were rather reluctant to give me permission at all. Last summer you know those two young men went over the ground with a mine detector and there was a story about them in one of the Boston papers. Apparently the family was snowed under with requests like mine at the time. They're rather fed up with the business but of course they've hung on to the land hoping something...I suppose they will get the money?"

"I imagine so. When it's found."

Wren sighed. "Well, they've waited long enough. I don't suppose I should be disappointed. I've only been engaged on it a few months. But you know I do feel I was headed in the right direction. I shall be tremendously interested to hear where and how it was located."

"So will I, for that matter," Jupiter admitted. "But I'd like to hear what you've done."

Pleased by this interest, Dr. Wren opened the book on the kitchen table. "First of all, as perhaps you know, there are some sixty acres of land that Potter owned at the time of his death, a rather large area to cope with, you must admit. Fortunately, like most of the land hereabouts, there are numerous stone walls breaking it up into smaller sections. Here on this page is a map of the entire piece showing the walls crisscrossing through it. That's on a scale of one square inch to an acre. As far as I've been able to ascertain about forty acres were cleared when he died. These are shown on the next page in green. They were mostly in permanent pasture but some were plowed and planted each year. You see ... May I get you another drink?"

Jupiter nodded and while Wren was preparing it he flipped through the notebook. There was a separate, carefully drawn map for each wall-enclosed lot and each one was numbered and its area indicated. There were nineteen of them and the largest appeared to be about five acres. "You've really gone into it, Doctor," Jupiter said, sighing.

"I've tried to put some system into it. It would be hopeless any other way. Remember there have certainly been at least one or two people continually engaged on the project for the last seventy years."

148

"What does the Potter family amount to these days?"

"Hiram and Beth had one son, William, who died in 1924. He married and had two children, a boy and a girl, who are still living. The son, William, Junior, lives in Portland, Maine, and it was he who gave me the authority to go over the ground. I understand the daughter is living on the West Coast."

"What about the factory Hiram owned? I suppose that was looked into?"

"Thoroughly."

"Where did Tom get hold of the diary he mentioned in his article?"

"From the son. He let me see it too and I had it photostated. Would you like to see it? It's very dull reading, except for the six poems, of course. Mostly notes on the weather, Hiram's health, his trips to Boston, and the buying and selling of farm animals. Naturally it has been examined many times by cryptographists who have found absolutely nothing."

"What about the couplets? Was the old boy really that active?"

"Who can tell? They certainly seem out of place in the diary and they have been the object of a great deal of attention, I can assure you. If they do refer to a code it has never been broken and I can't believe a simple shoemaker—that's what he was, of course, before he started his factory—could invent a code that couldn't be broken down."

"I suppose not. What are your theories?"

Bobbing under the beams, Wren returned with the drinks and sat down at the table. "That's just what they are. Theories. I've tried to put myself in Hiram's place. Tried to visualize the land as it must have looked to him, all that. Well, my first theory is that Potter would not have hidden the gold all at one time. One doesn't accumulate ninety thousand dollars, keep it around the house, and then bury it. Therefore he either had one place for it that could be reached when he wished to add to his store or he accumulated it in set sums and disposed of it separately. Do you follow?"

"Uh, huh."

"Now I further believe the location or locations he chose must have been relatively easy for him to find. I have proceeded on a theory I call Logical Landmarks. On each of the little maps of the separate lots you'll find these landmarks indicated. They are large boulders, the four corners of each lot, large trees, or any special or unusual construction in the wall itself."

"Good Lord," Jupiter said, awed. "There must be hundreds of places."

"So far I have indicated one hundred and seventy-two of them. However, most of these can be eliminated because they have already been explored. For example, there are eight large glacial boulders on the place and out from each of these the ground has been dug to a distance of fifty feet or more. Likewise the corners of each lot. Fortunately the family kept a careful record of what was done and I have that information."

"Have you done any digging yourself?"

"I've dug in eleven places so far. You'll find them marked in red on the maps."

"That must be hard work."

"It is but I've taken it in small doses. I never dig until I've convinced myself I've found a new Logical Location. It's rather exciting, you know. Great sport for a man with time on his hands. I . . . It's very hard for me to realize it's over."

Listening to him Jupiter became excited, too. He had respect for Wren's scientific method and wondered now if his own snap judgment about Arnold and the bottle of whiskey had been a good one. Logically if anyone had discovered the treasure it should have been the dentist and yet he didn't act like a man who had just turned up ninety thousand dollars in gold. He had been surprised and choked on his drink because Jupiter had stumbled on his secret hobby.

On the other hand if the gold *had* been found it would be almost too coincidental for Wren to have been in the freezer and not been involved in its discovery. Still Arnold had been looking for the money for thirty years and his chances were certainly as good as Wren's. Suppose Arnold had found it, how long would he be able to keep the discovery to himself? How, for example, would he go about converting the gold from bars or coin into cash? Would he try to do it by himself or wouldn't he be more likely to ask someone questions about the proper procedure and thus give himself away? Suppose he had asked Harry Dexter and Dexter had become curious and discovered Arnold had the gold. Wouldn't that be a better explanation of their "fight" yesterday morning, an argument someone might have witnessed and Dexter was anxious to explain away?

There was Mrs. Madison to be considered also. Tom had written the article and presumably there had been some discussion of the treasure between them. And then, of course, there was Maney who'd had, according to Joe, at least a passing interest in the subject.

Jupiter finished his drink and stood up, cautiously this time, remembering his head. "I'll let you know when anything definite develops, Doctor. The main thing now is to catch up with Arnold."

"Of course. Yes. You can understand how curious I am."

"I certainly can. It looks as if Tom's article might have started a gold rush in town."

Sighing, the doctor closed his notebook.

14

The afternoon had become rather warm and with the two drinks adding their bit Jupiter was tempted, when leaving the Wrens', to seek out a lawn and lie in the sun for a time under the pretext of doing some serious thinking. But since he realized the townspeople might misinterpret such an action on the part of the Chief of Police he drove along to the fire station to check his organization. He found them disposed in this fashion: two were listening to the ball game on a car radio, two were dispiritedly pitching horseshoes, one was kibitzing the game, and Ginger was asleep under the pumper. Except for the assorted guns stacked along the wall of the fire house it appeared to be a normal spring Saturday afternoon in Saxon.

After learning that the game was scoreless in the second and Williams was nothing for one, Jupiter went across the street to Vito's.

"I fin' out where he buy da bot," Vito said, omitting the ritual this time.

"I thought you would."

"One, two, t'ree, four, fivea places I call. They t'inka I'm crazy but I tell 'em I worka for da Chiefa da Police. He buy da bot in Hanley. Thursday, six o'clock."

"Fine. Nice work, Vito. Now why did he buy it?"

"Thassa right, Boss. Why? Some funny biz going on. You laugh, ha ha, when I tell you, I betcha what. Innian fin' da Potter money!"

"Ha, ha," Jupiter said. "What nonsense."

Vito squinted at him. "You t'inka so already, huh?"

"If he found the money why didn't he clear out with it? Would you go on living in a shack if you had ninety thousand dollars in gold?"

"Me? I go to Florida, smokea beeg cigar. Innian not so smart. He fin' gold, hafta ask someone what he do now. Pretend he ain't gotta da money when he ask."

"And the person he asks figures out he must have it, demands a share of it, and Arnold tries to kill him?"

"Thassa what I figure. Likea dat."

"Who? It would have to be one of the four people in the freezer. Maney?"

"Not him."

"Dexter?"

"Aah! He'sa too beeg-hearted."

"Dr. Wren?"

"Innian don' likea him."

"Don't tell me he'd go to Mrs. Madison?"

"She'sa one, Boss! Innian work for her, twenny years. She got money. He aska her."

"You want me to believe Mrs. Madison would try to work out a deal with Arnold? Risk going to jail?"

Vito shook his head vigorously. "No! Not likea dat! She mad at him. Shake her finger, say, 'Arn', you fin' money, gotta give him up. Don' belong to you.' Innian think I dumb aska her, now I gotta kill her."

"Not so good, Vito. Why hasn't Mrs. Madison said something about it?"

"She know Innian 'round there las' night?"

"My God! Maybe she doesn't! Neither Dexter nor Wren knew he was there!"

"You go ask her. Fin' out." Vito was very pleased with himself.

"I will. You're hot today, Vito. Where did Arnold find the gold and where is it now?"

"Ha. Ha. You want me do all work. You Chiefa da Police. Thassa one for you!"

Outside he met Tom Madison just coming out of Ginny's.

"Oh, hi, Jupe," Tom said smiling. "Come on in, we've got some news we want you to hear."

Apparently he hadn't been home to shave or change his clothes as yet; Jupiter followed him into the store where Ginny stood, her eyes shining, among her wares.

"Ginny and I are getting married," Tom said, proudly.

"On Wednesday," Ginny said. "We just decided this minute!"

"Wonderful!" Jupiter said. "Congratulations!"

Ginny laughed, looking at Tom. "And we weren't going to tell anyone!"

"Well, Jupe won't tell anyone. Will you?"

"Certainly not."

"And after all he's partly responsible," Tom said.

"How's that?" Jupiter asked.

"You convinced me I should give up the magazine."

"Hey, now wait a minute..."

"It's okay. I should have done it long ago, I know that now. I'm going to go to work for Ginny."

"We're going to be partners," Ginny said firmly. "He's been doing most of the buying for me anyway and the whole of the catalogue and—"

"The main thing is we can make a living out of it now and I'll bet in a few years..."

Jupiter was genuinely touched by their enthusiasm; it had been some years, he realized, since he had witnessed at first hand the heady optimism of young love triumphant. Evidently their plans included a home, a small but "very modern" house that Tom would erect with his own hands out of cement blocks. Jupiter gave his unqualified approval of everything and in a little while Tom left for his office on some urgent mission connected with the demise of the *Moderator.*

"Once he makes up his mind he's a ball of fire, isn't he?" Jupiter said.

Ginny's eyes filled up. "My, how I do love him! I've loved him since I was in the first grade."

"Oh, come now," Jupiter said, feeling he had to maintain some sort of standard.

"It's true. Really. The very first day at school I tore my dress at recess and I cried. He came up to me and said it didn't matter. He was in the third grade. Ever since then..." She got out a handkerchief. "I don't care! If you only knew! He went away to school, you know, to a private school and summers to camp. I used to walk up and down in front of his house when he was home and I'd wait in the post office and here, when Dad had the store. I used to almost die, really, when I saw him. Then at the dances, Christmas and holidays, if he should dance with me..."

She blew her nose thoroughly. "Well, you made it, Ginny," he said.

"Yes. I guess I've made it. Do you know why I came back to Saxon and started the store? It was because Tom came back here after the Army and started the magazine. I hadn't seen him or heard from him for three years. Well, it's worked out. By gosh, I think it has!"

"It certainly calls for something in the nature of a celebration. Maybe Betty and I can cook up a modest prenuptial festival early next week. Dinner in town, flowers, dancing girls . . ."

She laughed. "I suppose it's wrong to be so happy today. I mean . . . Well, you know if this hadn't happened, last night, I mean." She reflected for a moment, not smiling. "His mother made an awful mistake, accusing us, didn't she? I guess I'm getting Tom sort of on the rebound."

"Nobody ever got anybody any other way. We start rebounding at birth, Ginny."

"Well. Maybe that's true. Anyway she can't do anything now. I know she can't." She looked up at him, worried. "Can she?"

"No. You've had her on the ropes for some time. That was a desperation punch she threw last night and I'm certain she regrets it today. Has she been to the village yet do you know?"

"I don't think so. Why?"

"Just wondering. You can handle Tom from here but he won't get over his mother trouble all at once, remember. He's bound to backslide from time to time."

"Do you think getting married without letting her know is a good idea?"

"Is that the scheme?"

"Tom thought it would be best."

"He may be right. Anyway if I'd been in love since the first grade I think I'd get married and worry later."

158

"That's about the way I look at it. Thanks."

"Don't thank me, I haven't had any part in this. I don't even know it's happening."

A customer arrived and Jupiter departed. From across the street came a mild cheer. Williams had homered.

15

While the Wrens' was the oldest, the Madisons' brick-ended colonial was generally considered the most beautiful house in Saxon and it dominated the village green in much the manner that the Madison family had dominated town affairs in years past. It was doubtful, Jupiter reflected walking up to the handsomely fanlighted front door, if old Hiram Potter himself, for all his shrewd Civil War profiteering, had ever been invited here for a meal.

He opened the screen door, knocked, and waited. Nothing happened and he knocked some more. Backing away to get a better view of the fanlight he noticed the hall light inside was burning. This struck him as unusual in the extreme and he went up and tried the door. It was unlocked and he went in. In the living room he admired the Queen Anne furniture and a collection of Sandwich glass and went on through the dining room to the kitchen where he admired the inevitable deep freeze. He came back into the front hall, found the proper switch, and turned off the overhead light. A graceful staircase invited him to the second floor and he went up, making no attempt to muffle his footsteps. One door of the rooms leading off the upper hall was partly closed and he went to that and pushed it open. Mrs. Madison, with one bare arm outside of the covers, was lying, apparently asleep, in a canopied, four-poster bed. From the doorway he watched her for a moment and saw, with some relief, that she was breathing. Then, telling himself he was after all the Chiefa da Police, he walked in.

On her night table was a nearly empty bottle of sleeping pills and under it a note which he read:

> I can never, never forgive myself, Tom, my darling, for the horrible things I said tonight. Perhaps some day you can find it in your heart to forgive me.

He touched her hand quickly, on the chance he had made a mistake about her breathing, but it was warm. He found her pulse and counted it. It struck him as being a bit faster than normal. She remained motionless except for the rhythmic rising and falling of the blanket on her chest. Her gray hair was neatly combed out and lay unmussed on the pillow.

Jupiter lifted the small bottle, drew out the note, folded it carefully, and put it in his

161

pocket. He looked around the room, saw a sewing basket, went to it, and found a needle. With the needle in his fingers he came back to the bed, lit a match on his trousers, and sterilized the needle in the flame. Then he blew out the match and sat down on the edge of the bed.

"Where will you have it, madam?" he asked, conversationally.

She didn't move and Jupiter sighed. He reached into his pocket, brought out a penny, put the penny on his thumb, and placed the eyed end of the needle up against the penny, holding the needle between the tips of his first two fingers. With his free hand he held her wrist and pushed the needle an inch into her arm. Her body went rigid, she opened her eyes, and he withdrew the needle.

"You would have it," he said.

She moaned. "Tom . . . Tom, dear . . ."

Jupiter got up from the bed and sat down in a chair. She brought her hand to her head, covering her eyes. "Oh Tom . . . Tom . . . Is that you, Tommy?" She removed her hand and looked at him.

"That was fair," he said. "Would you like to take it again from the time when I came in the door?"

"I . . . I don't understand . . . What . . ."

"How many pills did you take, Mrs. Madison? Two? Three at the outside?"

She pulled herself slowly upright holding the blanket at her throat. Her eyes moved to the table where the note had been and then she faced him, her rage out of control at last.

"Get out! Give me that paper and get out!"

"That's better." He stood up, tossed her a bed jacket from the foot of the four-poster, and sat down again.

"I shall call the police!"

"Hm. Yes, you could try that, I suppose. But think about it a little before you do."

"You swine! You insolent swine!" She seemed to be gaining some control over herself now. She reached for the bed jacket and slipped it on. "You'll regret this moment, Mr. Jones! You'll regret it to your dying day!"

"Possibly. But this is an odd situation, Mrs. Madison. It's probably one of the few times in your life when your money, your social position, and, let me add, your courage aren't going to do you the least bit of good."

She was breathing very hard and he wondered idly how high her pulse rate had gone in the last few moments.

"I shall see you behind bars if it takes every ...everything I have! You broke into my house, you've stolen..."

"That's a point we ought to take up right away," he interrupted. "I don't know how long you've been feigning suicide up here but things have been happening this morning. Have you heard about Howland?"

In spite of herself she was interested in this. "Howland?"

"Howland is dead."

"I don't believe that." It was almost a whisper.

"As you like. At any rate I've been duly appointed to fill his position and it was in that capacity I entered your house. I knew Tom hadn't been here since last night and when I noticed your hall light burning downstairs I...Have you a question?"

"What do you want?" She was frightened now. "What do you want with me? Is it about Tom?"

He bowed his head to her. "Now, Mrs. Madison, you speak like a mother. A normal mother. No, it isn't about Tom. Tom's fine. Fortunately he missed finding you. Otherwise I doubt if he'd be so fine."

"Why did you come here?"

"I came here, as it happens, to ask you a very simple question."

"What is that?"

"Did you know Arnold, the Indian, was around the Maneys' barn last night?"

"Arnold? Whatever..."

"As ridiculous as it sounds I stick to the question. Did you know he was there?"

"No."

"You can't think of any reason he might have for wanting to kill you? Any reason at all?"

"Certainly not. He has worked for us for... What has Arnold...?"

"Howland was shot in Arnold's cabin. Arnold has disappeared."

He stood up, lit a cigarette, went to a window, pulled up the shade, and looked out. From there he could see the main street as far down as the fire station. The horseshoe game was still in progress. Mrs. Madison stirred in her bed but said nothing. While he was watching, Tom came out of his office over the station and crossed the street, presumably on his way to Ginny's.

"Aside from the relationship itself what have you got against Ginny as a daughter-in-law?" he asked, going back to his chair by the bed.

She looked at him steadily but her breathing was still very rapid. "If you'll destroy that note and leave my house, I give you my word I'll take no action against you."

"Sorry."

"Have you any idea how difficult I could make things for you and your wife and your children here in Saxon?"

"No, as a matter of fact, I haven't. What would you do, spread rumors about us?"

"You have lived here three years, Mr. Jones, and in that time I have learned quite a good deal about you. I make it my business to learn about new people."

Jupiter had naturally been aware for some time that he was dealing with an odd personality but he had not fully realized until this moment the extent of her aberration. She was undoubtedly a paranoiac, possibly dangerous if pressed too far, and certainly beyond his help.

The great difficulty lay in the fact that, as yet, she had committed no overt act which would justify her removal from society. She had simply, over the years, gone merrily on affecting, if not destroying, the lives of the victims of her capricious delusions. He recalled the ministers and the teachers reported to have suffered from her power and he thought also of Tom and Ginny. This was licensed madness, common enough in the world today, but how did one meet it? Did one always, forever and forever, give way before it? Was it enough to understand and forgive and make provision?

Certainly to the world at large and quite possible to a majority of professional psychiatrists pressed for a decision, this woman was rational enough to be free. Was he at liberty then to meet her on her own terms?

He got up again and went to a different window. From this one he could see the Unitarian church and beyond it the tiny parsonage. The minister was in his yard planting a box of pansies.

"If you do not give me that paper and leave this house within one minute I shall run out into the street as I am and call for help!"

"Will you accuse me of rape or hadn't you thought of that?" He remained at the window, thinking. Finally he said, "You went too far last night, Mrs. Madison. You drove Tom straight to Ginny. Even if he'd found you just now you couldn't hold him for long. But you were right to try and play on his sympathies, that's where your strength lies. If you don't want Tom to despise you for the rest of your life, you'd better listen to me now."

He didn't look toward the bed and in a moment she said, "I'll give you five minutes. No more."

"The values you stand for and have worked to preserve are being threatened on every hand today, Mrs. Madison. You have a tradition of culture, of integrity, of responsibility to the community that musn't be destroyed. This town owes the Madisons and you personally a debt it could never repay. It must often seem to you we are ungrateful." From the bed there was a barely audible sigh but he did not as yet dare to look at her. "You're quite right in thinking Ginny is a threat to those values, the values you've given to Tom. She is beneath him, not in the old-fashioned sense of mere class distinction, but in the richness, the variety, the depth of his heritage." He moved away from the window, looked quickly and saw she was staring up at the canopy, and stopped at a small writing table. There was an open box of notepaper lying there and as he talked he carefully lifted out a sheet and, keeping his back to the bed, folded it as he had folded the suicide note in his pocket. "Tom has been blinded by her two most dangerous weapons—her youth and her availability. You've done everything in your power to save him. You've done things lesser women, lesser mothers, would not have had the courage to do." He paused and waited.

"I . . . Go ahead, Mr. Jones."

"Right now you're angry at me, justifiably so, under the circumstances. I felt it was necessary to shock you into listening to me. For Tom's sake and yours. You mustn't turn him against you, Mrs. Madison. He needs your love and his trust in you. Now more than ever before."

"If I could believe you really understood . . ."

"I do understand. Believe me." He went quickly to the bed, slipping the empty paper into his pocket on the way. Her mouth was still a firm line but he could see confusion and the beginning of trust in her eyes. He risked sitting down on the edge of the bed. "You have fought this alone, knowing the whole town was against you in it. Only the very brave fight lonely battles, Mrs. Madison." She turned her head away and tears came into her eyes. "But the greatest test of the brave is when they must ask for help."

"What shall I do?" It was a whisper.

He took her hand. "You must keep Tom's love. He must never be deprived of your guidance and counsel. It may be that he'll marry Ginny. It may be you should direct him to marry her." He felt her stiffen and went on quickly. "Think about it a minute. Think what it will mean if he is married to her. Can she match your unselfish devotion to him? The devotion of a lifetime? Won't her very lack of the high values you have given him turn him back toward you? How long will it take before his eyes are opened to her inferiority? Yes, you'd try and spare him this awakening, that's natural in a devoted mother. But often drastic surgery is required to save the body as a whole. In your heart you know you must steel yourself to promote this unhappy marriage and cut out the cancer of Tom's misdirected love. It'll be hard for you but you must welcome this girl into your home. You must summon all your strength to remain gracious to her in Tom's eyes. Perhaps only a woman with your great courage, your high heritage, and your unsparing love could bring herself to make such a sacrifice but I feel this is what you must try to do." Afraid he might have gone a bit overboard on the thing, he brought out the blank sheet of folded notepaper and showed it to her. "This must always remain a secret between us, Mrs. Madison." He tore the paper in half, put the two pieces together and tore it again.

"I'm afraid I've misunderstood you, Mr. Jones."

He lifted an ashtray from the bed table, dropped the pieces of paper into it, and struck a match. "I want you to know you'll always have one friend, one admirer here in Saxon. I know what you must have suffered to have done this thing." He lit the paper and as she watched it burn, her eyes brimming over, he wondered if at that instant she could be persuading herself that she had actually tried to commit suicide. He put the ashtray back on the table and took her hand again. He toyed with the idea of kissing it but felt he shouldn't press his luck too far.

"I have always tried to do what was right for Tom," she said, returning the pressure of his hand. "I must think if what you say is right."

"Do think about it, my dear. You have so very much to give him."

"I suppose I knew all along it must come to this but I have been so upset..."

"I know the strain you've been under. Just now you owe yourself some consideration. Get up, get dressed, and walk out into the sunshine. Think for once of your own life, your own happiness." He pressed her hand once more and stood up. He smiled down at her and then, as if overcome by his emotion, quickly turned his head away and walked from the room.

Back at the fire station the ball game was tied up, 2–2, in the fifth.

"Only the fifth?" he said. "I can't believe it."

Well, he had proved something, he supposed. Vito's theory was wrong and, in the note, he had a rather valuable wedding present for Ginny. He decided to drive out to the Maneys'. Slim's sanity would be refreshing.

16

At the Maneys' the day's drinking had begun in earnest. Slim, Joe, and Maney, all with high-balls, were in the barn while Detective McCoy and Troopers Kearns and Porter, without high-balls, but with admiring side glances at Slim, were watching the ball game on the new television set, temporarily installed on top of the bar.

"Mix the Chief a drink, lad," Maney said to Joe. "I'm sure *he'll* take a drink on duty."

"It's not that, Mr. Maney," McCoy protested. "I just don't go for the stuff any time."

"You ought to," Maney said. "It'd sharpen your wits. Take Chief Jones, I'll wager he's got this business pretty well doped out already. What about that, Jonesy?"

"No comment," said Jupiter. "The detective gives out the statements."

"About that, Ed. Mr. Maney..."

"Mr. Maney nothing," Maney interrupted. "Mr. Maney said to handle it any way you wanted."

"A couple of news hawks were here," Joe explained. "They just left to examine the scene."

"Detective McCoy told them Arnold had been seen in Boston," Maney said. "He has a lively imagination."

"I did what I thought was best all around, Mr. Maney. I..."

"It doesn't matter very much," Jupiter broke in. "You may be able to pick him up tonight."

He explained about the swamp and Arnold's lady friend.

"That's the break we've been waiting for," McCoy said, rubbing his hands. "Come on, boys, let's get to work on this!"

"Now he's all business," Maney said when McCoy and the troopers had left. "He'd have sat here all day on his fat—"

"Your wife phoned a while ago," Joe called to Jupiter, from behind the bar. "She didn't say what she wanted. Just wondered if you were here."

"Make it weak, Joe," Jupiter said. "I suppose I'd better call her."

"Right here." Bateman put a telephone on the bar. When Jupiter walked up to it Joe nodded quickly at Maney and whispered, "Drunk and ugly. Watch it." And then, normally, "All the comforts of home."

Jupiter gave his number to the operator. Maney was lying on the wheeled chaise longue, holding his drink on his chest. Slim, looking oddly preoccupied, was at the piano picking out tunes with one finger.

"Hi," Jupiter said when Betty answered.

"Hi."

"I'm at Maney's."

"Having fun? I keep feeling I'm missing something."

"We're just watching the ball game on the video."

"Our video?"

"I don't know about that."

While Jupiter was watching him, Maney reached in his pocket and brought out a small flat automatic. He opened it up, examined the full clip, and put it back in his pocket.

Betty said, "Looks as though Parnell really has it today, although they touched him up a little there in the third."

"Yes," Jupiter said. "Was there anything special on your mind?"

"No...Oh, yes. You know Tom's article on the pot o' gold?"

"Uh, huh."

"I just read it again. Those poems. I'll bet they're a clue."

"They could be. I understand they've been studied pretty thoroughly by experts though."

"Have they really? I thought I was being quite bright. I even read them aloud to the children to get their opinion. Oh, well."

"How did they like them?"

"Susan was fascinated by the ladies' names.

When I told her they were old-fashioned she said: 'Yes, I know. Like you see on gravestones.' Do you think our children are morbid? Do they listen to the radio too much?"

"No. Life is like that. Life is morbid."

"Oh, dear. Is Slim being mean to you? Doesn't she love you today like she did last night?"

He smiled. Now he knew why she'd called him. "More than ever."

"Oh, I am glad of that. You deserve having a big, beautiful, long-legged blond girl chasing after you. It's little enough."

"I try to think of it that way."

"Be kind to her, lover."

"I shall."

"No, you can't speak to Daddy! Good-by!"

He hung up and sipped his drink.

"Nothing unimportant, I trust," Joe said.

"Could, to coin a phrase, be."

"Don't start that, Jonesy," Joe warned, smiling. "It's habit forming."

"What's habit forming?" Maney demanded.

"Fooling around with clichés. We banished it this morning, remember?"

"So, as you say, we did." Maney chuckled happily to himself. "Did you like that one, Jonesy?"

"See?" Joe said. "He can't leave it alone."

The Red Sox got two men aboard in the seventh but nothing came of it and the score remained tied.

"Baseball, shmaseball." Slim got up from the piano and stretched. "I'm gonna take Stardust for a ride."

"No, you don't," Maney said quickly. "You don't go off the place while that Indian stays loose."

"Is that what the gun's for?" Jupiter asked as lightly as he could.

"That's just what it's for, Jonesy. How do I know that crazy bastard won't decide to come gunning for me? He knows I sent Howland after him last night."

"That's a point," Jupiter admitted.

"You're damn well told it's a point."

"How about just in the paddock, Jack, honey?" Slim asked. "Jonesy can come along and protect me."

"Maybe Jonesy wants to talk to the boss," Joe said quickly. "I'll go with you. I'm expendable. Besides, my birds require attention."

"Okay, then," Slim said. "Come along, stupid."

They went out. "Have a seat," Maney suggested and Jupiter left the bar and sat down. "I don't get this business, Jonesy. I can't figure it at all."

It appeared that Maney might be sincerely frightened but whether it was on account of the chance that Arnold would show up or for some other reason he was unprepared to guess. When Maney brought his glass to his mouth Jupiter was tempted to repeat the test he had used on Dr. Wren but rejected it on esthetic grounds. Like Mrs. Madison, he mused, I have my standards.

"What could the bastard have against any of us? Have you got anywhere at all with it?"

"Not far. Harry had a squabble with Arnold yesterday but..."

"Harry? What was that about?"

When Jupiter had told him Maney swore. "Can you beat that guy? He's all hot and bothered about Slim, too. Did you know about that?" Jupiter nodded and Maney explained in some detail what he believed was the matter with Dexter. Unlike Jupiter's psychological diagnosis Maney's was mainly anatomical. It was an ugly and vicious attack and Jupiter was thankful Joe had apprised him of Maney's condition in time. Otherwise he might have decided to take yet another moral stand. He would allow himself the exception today of not tangling intellectually with armed drunks.

"You seen the others? Wren and Mrs. Madison?"

"Yes. They say Arnold has nothing against them."

"You figure someone's lying?"

"It looks that way."

Maney took a long swallow, then half-smiled at Jupiter. "You figure it might be me?"

"That's a hell of a question. Sure. It might be you."

"You're a hot one, Jonesy," Maney said and

laughed. "Sometimes I have you tagged as a long-haired phony and then sometimes I don't know. What the hell is this book you're writing?"

"Mostly theories about art and life. None of it's particularly original. It's a rehash to get my name in print."

"Yeah, but what's it about?"

"Well, to be honest, it's a pretty special field."

"Meaning I'm too uneducated to understand it, huh?"

"That's right," Jupiter said easily. "You'd find it as tough going as I'd find a book on atomic fission. All these special fields have a language of their own."

Maney shook his head slowly. "That's what gets me about you. Right there. I get set for you to weasel or brush me off and I get a straight answer that makes sense. Are you a Commy, Jonesy?"

Jupiter laughed. "Think of me as a phony but not that."

"I wouldn't give a damn if you were. At least those bastards believe in something. What do you believe in, Jonesy?"

Well, Jupiter thought, how am I going to get out of this one?

"Do you mean what are my politics?"

"No. Hell, no. What's it all about? What makes it tick?"

Fortunately, at that moment, there was diversion from the television set. It was now the eighth and Williams was up with a man on first. The serious talk was postponed until Ted flied out deep to left, retiring the side.

"I don't see why he tries that," Maney complained. "He ought to plaster 'em all to right."

Secretly Jupiter agreed with this but he said, "I don't know. He gets a lot of hits that way."

"Aah," said Maney. "He's a tough one to figure, too. That Williams."

"Do you know him?"

"Sure. I know all those boys. But, listen, Jonesy, what keep a smart guy like you from shooting yourself?"

"Baseball, for one thing."

"No. That answer's no good."

"The question's no good."

Maney finished off his drink and swore. "I'm getting so stiff I can't think straight. You know what I mean."

"Okay. I'll give you an answer. I believe we're living in a very rough age where there aren't any big, handy answers. I don't believe it will keep on like this indefinitely but in the meantime I think a man has to do the best he can with what he's got around him. I think we're forced into limited objectives and the old-fashioned, simple disciplines, say the Golden Rule or the Boy Scout oath. At least that's the way I'm operating at the moment."

"Yeah. In other words you don't believe in anything."

"Certainly I do. I take quite a lot largely on

faith. For instance I believe mankind is readily capable of organizing a sane world for itself. I just don't see any sign of it happening. Nothing I'd care to back with a dollar."

"What would you back with a dollar?"

"That I won't answer now. I'm a police officer with a limited objective. We'd be here all night." He stood up. "I want to have another look around your basement if you don't mind. I want to see if I can figure out where Arnold was when you all went downstairs."

"Fix me a drink while you're up, huh?"

"Sure."

When he came back with the highball, Maney winked. "What'll you give I'm the liar?"

"Ninety thousand to one."

Maney frowned. "I don't get that."

"Then that changes the odds. You're about even money, Jack."

"You're a slick one, Jonesy. I do declare."

He left him shaking his head and went downstairs. In the packaging room outside the freezer he noticed the padlock was back in place and then he walked over and looked at the door that led out to the garage, the one behind which Arnold had been listening the night before. He opened it and rapped the paneling; it was lightly constructed and the Indian had probably been able to hear voices through it. He went into the garage and closed the door behind him. There was a keyhole in the door and it was conceivable Arnold had, as he said, seen light through it, although the door itself fitted tightly enough in its frame. But Arnold certainly couldn't have been in here when Maney and the others had come down on their tour, because Maney had shown them the new tractor and the Indian would have been discovered.

Jupiter went back through the packaging room and out into the open through the doorway he and Slim had entered from the stable. The ground here slanted sharply up across a narrow walk from the door and the one window of the packaging room. Arnold must have been on the walk just outside the window to have been able to see and recognize the people going into the freezer. From where he stood Jupiter looked along the barn and decided that anyone standing at the end could have seen Arnold in the light from the window. Unhappily, though, nobody had.

"So much for that," he muttered and climbed to the top of the embankment.

At the far end of the paddock Slim was riding bareback on Stardust. When she saw him she waved, put the horse into a canter, headed for the near fence, and took it with something to spare. It was graceful indeed but Jupiter's stomach turned over; he had no great love for or trust in horses. As they approached he retreated a few steps down the bank. She slid off, quickly removed the bridle, and slapped the horse on its rump. "G'wan home now." Remarkably, the animal obeyed.

"You're a big show-off," he said.

She didn't smile. "Didn't you know I wanted to talk to you, honey? When I said about goin' out for a ride?"

"I must have missed that one, Slim."

"Well, I did." Her lower lip was out and the preoccupied look he had noticed earlier was still there. Though novel, the effect was fetching enough. "C'mon down in here, Jonesy."

She led him back into the packaging room and shut the door softly.

"Jack still upstairs?" she whispered and when he nodded, "I feel just awful."

As he looked at her two large tears formed on her lower lids and hung there until she blinked them away. He felt he'd really had a surfeit of weeping females this day: first Ginny, then Mrs. Madison, and now Slim, of all people.

"I did an awful thing, Jonesy."

Suddenly and incredibly he knew what she was going to say. It was wildly implausible, and yet at the same damned time unremittingly logical. "*Oh, no, Slim.*"

"Uh, huh." Her chin quivered as she nodded and swallowed together. "It was me locked 'em in last night."

17

"Does Jack know?"

"Oh, no!" The frightened, about-to-be-punished look of a naughty little girl amused him but he didn't smile. "You wouldn't tell him? He'd be wild, Jonesy!"

"My God, Slim, don't you realize what..."

"Oh, I do! Honest. It was an awful thing to do but I didn't mean any harm. It was a joke, honey. Oh." She came up and put both hands on his arms. "It wasn't to hurt anyone, Jonesy."

"But you left them in there an hour!"

She shook her head. "It wasn't an hour, honest. Three quarters, only. I kept track. I tried it on myself so I knew."

"You what?"

"It was after Joe put on the padlock. When I got the idea. One day I stayed in there a whole hour and it didn't hurt me. I was goin' to do it sometime on Joe an' Jack. Then last night..." She put her forehead against his shoulder. "I didn't think anyone..."

"You didn't think anyone was going to get killed, I know," he said and put his hands on her shoulders. "But, dammit, Slim, last night when I asked you about it, out in the stable, I told you it would get messy. You knew those people thought someone had tried to kill them."

"I'm so dumb, Jonesy. I thought so long as no one *had* tried to kill them what harm would it do? I only did it because of the square dancing being so stupid. Then, when we found Howland...Oh, gee, Jonesy, I'm scared!"

She was trembling now and he patted her back abstractedly. Had Arnold, as he'd hinted, really seen her? Had Maney...?

"What'll I do, honey? It's like I killed Howland myself."

"Not quite. It was a poor joke, I'll admit, and I wish to hell you'd told me last night, but... I've got to think about this a little. It throws out the theory I've been working on...or does it?" Yes, of course, it must. Arnold must have seen her, must have thought more seriously of blackmailing Maney, must have talked to him again later last night, and then, when he got home, a car had come in and he'd loaded his shotgun ...But what about that bottle of whiskey? That was a fact, not a theory. "This is a mess, Slim."

"I wanted to tell you, Jonesy. I was never in trouble like this before and Jack..."

"I think you'll have to tell him, Slim. You should have told him before. Last night he was

183

sure you'd locked the door. He asked me to find out for him."

"He'd kick me out."

"Don't be silly. He'll understand about this. Hell, he got a great laugh out of your shooting him. You did shoot him on purpose, didn't you?"

"Uh, huh. But this is different, honest. This was real bad. He'd kick me out and then...and then I wouldn't have Stardust!"

Apparently the thought of this separation was too much for her and she sobbed. It was also a little too much for Jupiter and he said sharply, not whispering anymore, "Stop it, Slim! This is bad and a man has been killed but Jack's not likely to divorce you because of it!"

"He won't have to divorce me, honey," she said, sniffling. "We're not married."

Well, he thought, if this isn't a day for surprises! "You're not?" It was the best he could do.

"Uh, uh. He's married already. A long time ago, I mean. He can't get a divorce, you know, on account of his religion. So...Gee, I guess maybe I shouldn't've told you about that, Jonesy. Nobody knows, not even Joe!"

Jupiter took a deep breath, held it a moment, and then let it out slowly. He put his hand on her head. "How old are you, Slim?"

"Twenty-two. But it isn't like you think, honey. I've been married before myself. I was married when I was fifteen back home but my folks got it, you know, annulled. They did right, though. He was a bum."

"Was that when you went to New York?"

"Not then. I got married again. Not right after—four months, I think it was. He was a real nice kid. Jimmy."

"What happened to him?"

"He got killed. It was the war then. He was in training at a camp near home. Then he got shipped overseas. That's when I went to New York, when he was killed, I mean. The gov'ment gives you an allowance."

"Was Jimmy the one who taught you how to shoot?"

"Oh, no, Jonesy. How'd you know about that? That was another kid I went around with in New York for a while. It was in New York I met Jack. You know, when I was dancing."

"And Jack can't get a divorce?"

"That's right. That's why I say if he ever got mad at me, real mad, he could kick me out and..."

He held her close, as he might have held one of his own children bewildered by the ways of the world. "We'll work this one out, honey. You and me."

And then, shockingly, Maney himself was swaying at the foot of the stairs. "So, by Christ, this is it, huh? This is what I was trying to figure! Right on my own place! You and your Golden Rule, you..."

He put out a hand and steadied himself

against the wall. His heavy face was dead white, his mouth twisted in anger. And he brought out his automatic.

"Jack!"

"Shut up, you whore! Get away from him!"

Jupiter held Slim in his arms. "Take it easy, Maney. You can't beat a murder rap."

"Oh, no? Suppose I try?"

"What'll you plead, the unwritten law? You're not even married to this girl, you son-of-a-bitch."

The shock of it held him for an instant and Jupiter let Slim go. "Put that gun away." He moved toward the stairs.

Maney held up his left hand. "One more step and you get it."

Jupiter stopped, his hand out for the gun. "No, you don't, you bastard," Maney said. "You stay right where you are." His eyes, filled with hate, flicked quickly to Slim and back to Jupiter. His left hand went into his pocket and came out with a bunch of keys. He tossed them to Slim. "Open up that door, you little bitch. I think I'll just cool you two off."

Slim had not caught the keys. Now she bent down and picked them up. "Jack, honey, you got this..."

"*Open it up!*" He choked it out, saliva at one corner of his mouth.

She went to the freezer door, found the proper key, and unsnapped the padlock.

"Now get in there! Both of you!"

He left the stairs, his gun out, and Jupiter moved toward the door.

"All the way!"

He lurched forward and shoved Jupiter hard against Slim, so that they both stumbled into the freezer room. At the door Maney snapped on the inside light.

"Take a good look at each other. Go on, get it out of your goddam system!"

He slammed the door.

Slim turned to Jupiter, her eyes wide and wet, her handsome chest heaving.

"I guess I should've warned you, Jonesy," she said sadly out of the sudden cold silence that surrounded them. "Jack is an awful jealous man!"

18

"He's all of that," Jupiter said shortly. He braced himself and shoved against the door but it was locked. Maney wasn't playing any tricks.

"It'll be all right, honey. Joe'll get us out soon as he gets done with his birds."

"How'll he know we're in here?"

"Why..." She frowned and then she was suddenly frightened. "He will know, somehow, won't he, Jonesy?"

"Sure," he said quickly. "How long does he usually take with his birds?"

"Oh, gosh, I don't know. Sometimes he stays out there a long time, just lookin' at 'em. But Jack wouldn't..." She licked her lips quickly. "He wouldn't, would he?"

"You know him better than I do, Slim. Have you ever seen him as mad as that?"

"Oh, I've seen him mad but I don't think ever like that. You shouldn't have called him—you know—what you did."

"Possibly not."

The room was roughly fourteen feet square and, at this season, nearly empty. An adequate supply of frozen meat and vegetables was in evidence but there were only a dozen orange crates of pheasants piled along one wall. The birds were packed in pairs in red cardboard, Cellophane-topped cartons on which was written in script, "Compliments of Jack Maney." Jupiter pulled out a crate, set it on end, and sat down. The cold was already noticeable through his thin clothes. He thought, if Maney really wanted to leave them in here he couldn't have picked a better time for it. He could drive Jupiter's car off into the woods, bury them at his leisure when they were stiff and easy to handle, and the dirty work would be blamed on the Indian. He decided he'd better keep this thought to himself.

What a mess it was and what a mess he was making of it! He should have had sense enough last night to have gone after Slim about the padlock. He could have broken her down some way if he'd really thought about it but... Well, there was no use blaming himself now, he'd been in too much of a party mood like everyone else.

She was watching him miserably, her arms crossed, her hands clutching her shoulders. And he'd thought she was the one individual in all this he completely understood!

He sighed. "Tell me, that time you spent an

hour in here what did you do to amuse yourself?"

"I danced mostly," she said sadly. "You know, the routines from the shows. Like this." She put her elbows out as if linked in a chorus line, took two steps forward, and kicked. "That's how I kept warm, Jonesy."

He shook his head. Was anyone expected to make moral judgments about a girl like this? He stood up. "Teach me a routine, Slim. It's a skill I should have and we've got all the time in the world."

Solemnly she took his arm and for five minutes they stepped forward two, kicked, stepped to the left, kicked, stepped to the right, kicked, and back.

"You're doin' fine, honey!"

"It beats square dancing," he panted.

She began to sing. "'A pretty girl...kick!...is like a melody...kick!' That's it!"

He joined her in song for a few measures but then, winded, he stopped and sat down. Alone she did a cartwheel, ending with an authentic bump. "Ouch! That floor's cold on the hands!"

She smiled at him and shook her long hair back into place.

"I'll tell you something," he said, once more shaking his head. "You get my vote for the girl I'd most like to be locked up in a deep freeze with, Slim."

"Honest? You're not sore at me anymore?" She came over and sat on his lap. "It's not so bad in here after all, huh, Jonesy?" She put her arm around his neck. "I'll keep you warm, honey."

"I believe you. But there's a point that worries me. They claimed last night they were troubled by lack of oxygen. Maybe we ought to sort of ration ourselves. We were burning it up there pretty fast."

"Will we burn it up more because I'm sittin' on you?"

"No. This is a very efficient arrangement. But I was thinking..." He looked around at the cases. "You know what we really need, Slim?"

"Sure. I can think of a lot of things."

"Yes, but I don't see why we can't build us an igloo out of these crates. Get up a minute."

He pulled some crates away from a corner and studied the problem.

"What good will this do?" she asked, watching him.

"Conserve our hard-earned body heat. Like Eskimos. Sit down on the floor in the corner there. I want to try it for size."

From one wall, leaving space for himself beside her, he placed two crates lengthwise on the floor and then piled two more layers on top, staggering them in a little toward the corner.

"This'll be cozy, Jonesy. Only my bottom's getting cold."

"It'll warm up."

For a roof he tilted four crates the long way from the wall he'd built to the wall of the room.

It gave a rather pleasant gabled effect and he found he had just two crates left over for a door. He climbed in backwards on his knees and worked the two crates around until they covered the opening. It was hardly tight but it would serve.

"There," he said and squeezed back gingerly beside her. "We ought to get it up to thirty-two in here in no time."

"Gee, Jonesy, you're smart." She snuggled against him in the dark. "It's lucky you're thin, too. You don't take up much room."

"It's lucky you're pretty. I wouldn't do this with Mrs. Madison."

She giggled, was silent for a while, and then said, "You want to kiss me, honey?"

He'd felt the point was bound to come up sooner or later. "I'd like to kiss you but I don't want you to get any wrong ideas. I've been a faithful husband for eight years and I like it that way." He sighed. "I class this under a happy necessity." He kissed her and, during it, jarred the wall. "Maybe we'd just better rub noses, Slim, the roof almost fell in."

"You know something?" she asked thoughtfully, after a while.

"What?"

"I bet I could fall in love with you. You know, like we talked about last night. Like in books."

He took her hands, which were cold, and held them against his chest. "That would be a dumb thing to do and you're not a dumb girl."

"What if I couldn't help it?"

"You can help it. Tell me something. Is your father still running that drugstore back in Waco?"

"Uh, huh. Why?"

"What kind of a guy is he?"

"Oh, we got along all right, I guess. He was always foolin' around with some idea to get rich. You know, some medicine he was goin' to invent. Nothin' ever happened."

"What about your mother?"

"Oh, her. She's not so much, Jonesy. Still, I guess all she ever wanted was some fun out of life." She was silent for a moment. "I wouldn't go back there, if that's what you had in mind."

"What do you think you will do?"

"You mean if Jack kicks me out? I'd go to New York again, I guess. Only I'd sure enough miss Stardust."

"Suppose he doesn't kick you out?"

"Why then I'd stay right on here, of course. Honest, we have good times most always."

He wondered if there was any value in pursuing it farther. Suppose he could make her understand her true motive for shooting Maney and locking him up in here, would that help? Unhappily he couldn't produce what she needed, a husband and a home, out of a hat. It was clear she had accepted this abortive relationship with Maney because her first two marriages, through no fault of her own, had blown up. This was what her world had offered her and she had come to terms with it without complaint or protest, excepting, of course, these last two "jokes."

"Jonesy?"

"What?"

"Supposin' you weren't already married. Would you like me?"

"Though married, I like you."

"I mean am I the type girl you'd marry?"

"You sure are, Slim."

"No kiddin'?"

"On the level. You and Betty are a good deal alike."

"She's smarter'n me. She makes jokes all the time."

"Not all the time, fortunately. But you're prettier."

"You'd get sick of lookin' at me."

"That's a chance I'd take. But this is just talk, shmalk, Slim. You know that, don't you?"

"Uh, huh."

"Are you getting cold? Shall we dance?"

"No. I wonder where Joe is?"

He looked at his watch and saw they'd been inside for twenty minutes. "He'll be along."

But suppose Maney, in his drunken rage, had simply driven off somewhere? Or, if he was still upstairs, he should pass out before Joe got back from tending his pheasants? They could scream their heads off and pound on the walls but he would never hear them.

There was, Jupiter supposed, a certain justification, an explanation at least, for Maney's wild jealousy, beyond the simple fact that he had found them in each other's arms. Maney could accept the challenge of Joe's intelligence and personality because Maney did, after all, pay the bills, but Jupiter, a free agent, had unwittingly challenged him on the same grounds and, going much farther and still unwittingly, had seemed successfully to attack his manhood. Not for nothing had Joe warned him this morning to stay away from Slim. Sober, Jupiter doubted if Maney would even have threatened to kill them but, unhappily, he was far from sober.

"That Joe. Sometimes he gives me a pain."

"Why, Slim?"

"He's so lazy, honest. Take the piano. If he'd practice he could get real good and get a job with a band. I've told him. He says he can't even read music."

"Maybe he can't."

"Oh, he can't, I know that, but why shouldn't he learn to? Him. He'll never amount to anything."

There seemed to be some emotion here and Jupiter suddenly wondered if it would be possible for him to pull Joe out of the hat. Why not? He might be just the husband for her. What am I today, he silently demanded, a busybody or my brother's keeper? Does all wisdom reside in Edmund Jones? Certainly not, but enough perhaps for the problem at hand.

"I think I can tell you why Joe won't study the piano. It's not because he's lazy but because he knows he can never be first rate. He's listened to the good boys and he knows what it takes. That's a thing about Joe. He won't ever kid himself."

"Well, he could be good. Maybe not the best but, honest, Jonesy, he could be good."

"He's not ready to settle for that yet. He still wants to be best."

"My gosh, how can he be best if he won't even practice?"

"He won't commit himself to anything unless he can believe in it. He can't believe in himself as a piano player because he knows he can't be tops in it. So he leaves it alone. Probably the piano, now that you mention it, is as close as he's come to getting serious about anything."

She sniffed. "Sometimes he's serious enough about those ol' birds of his."

"That should show you he can be serious about something, but for a smart boy like Joe Bateman they aren't enough. He won't commit himself to raising pheasants. Maybe he'd do it for a living if he had anything else he could believe in."

"Such as?"

"Oh, the usual things," he said, offhandedly, "getting rich, doing good in the world, raising a family. Any one of those things."

She thought about this and then asked, "Do you really think he's so smart?"

"He's a pretty bright boy, Slim."

"Smarter than Jack?"

"In some ways. I have a hunch when Jack was Joe's age he was pretty well committed to getting rich. Now he's beginning to wonder how smart he was spending the best part of his life at it."

"Being rich is okay. Take it from me."

"It certainly is but I don't think Joe's ready to spend all his time at it. He'd settle for a decent living."

"Oh, well. I should worry about him. I'm cold, honey, let's shake it up a little, huh?"

Outside the igloo they repeated their weird but bracing routine and during it Jupiter allowed his mind to return to the problem of Arnold. What actually was changed by Slim's admission? Kick. Couldn't the Potter treasure somehow be involved? Kick. Could Slim's act have set off a chain of violence connected with it? If he only knew where the damned gold was buried, whether or not it had been dug up, he could . . .

"Kick, Jonesy!"

"Oh, sorry."

If he was any good at all he ought to be able to locate the stuff. Kick. What about Wren's Logical Locations? Had the old boy looked into them all? Kick. Wren was right, there must have been a simple hiding place or a series of them. If there was only a clue . . .

"Hey!" He stopped dancing.

"What's the matter?"

"We've got to get out of here, Slim!"

He ran to the door and pushed. It was still locked.

"Take it easy, honey," she said, worriedly. "It's okay. We're doin' okay."

"But dammit, Slim, I think I've solved this thing! I've got to get out and see if I'm right!"

"But, Jonesy, you can't get out till Joe comes."

"Where is that guy? Hell, there must be a way to get out of here!"

He looked around, his eye stopping at last on the light bulb over the door. "Maybe. Maybe. You wouldn't know if this is on the circuit upstairs?" And when she shook her head, "No, of course, you wouldn't. It might be, though. It's a chance to take. Joe could be up there watching television. I'm going to blow a fuse, Slim. It'll be dark in here but it might just work."

He reached up, removed the bulb, brought his penny out of his pocket, put it in the socket, and screwed the bulb back in.

"There goes the fuse."

He removed the bulb and the penny and once more put the bulb back in.

"If that should go on again we're as good as out. I can keep blowing fuses until Joe traces the trouble into here."

"Gee!"

"Learned that in prep school, Slim. Sometimes it pays to get an education." He lit a match. "Let's return to our nest and wait and see if it works."

He was still holding the match and she was on her knees backing into the igloo when the door opened, lighting the room. Joe was there, alone.

"Gosh, Jonesy, it certainly worked!" she exclaimed happily.

"Couldn't have worked that fast," he told her and turned to Joe. "How's the coast? Clear?"

Bateman nodded, not smiling. "You ought to have your head examined, Jones, I told you not to fool around."

"No one was fooling around. Where's Maney?"

"I put him to bed." As they came out of the freezer he looked at them angrily. "If you two weren't fooling around what got him so crazy mad?"

"Slim locked the door here last night," Jupiter said. "She was telling me about it when Jack found us."

Bateman swore and faced Slim. "How stupid can you get?"

"Relax, Joe," Jupiter said. "She's explained it satisfactorily to me."

"What the hell do you mean?" He whirled on Jupiter, his jaw out. "I don't get this at all! Jack didn't say anything about her locking the door. He said he found you two down here necking! It's damned lucky he didn't shoot you both!"

"I agree about that. Did he tell you we were in here?"

"Yeah. Finally. I knew something was wrong when he said you'd gone for a walk. Then he decided to drive to Boston but I wouldn't let him get in the car. I had to slug him to stop him. That's when he told me where you were. The poor bastard's out of his head. But he's asleep now."

It was plain Joe felt a deep sense of loyalty toward Maney but though Jupiter respected it he was also in a hurry. "Did you know Slim and Jack weren't married?"

"Honest, Jonesy, I..." Slim began.

Jupiter held up his hand, watching Joe. "He's been married for some time to another woman. He told Slim he couldn't get a divorce."

"I...I don't believe it," Bateman said.

"Well, it's true," Slim said. "But I don't see what's so wrong about it. I knew what I was doin'."

Joe took a deep breath, all the hostility gone from his face, then he looked at Slim, slowly shaking his head. "You beautiful dope." He swallowed and turned to Jupiter. "It's funny. I figured I knew all there was to know about that guy."

"That's always dangerous," Jupiter said, "when you're dealing with people."

"Yeah. But two years I've known him! How many times have I been plastered with him, I wonder? A thing like that!"

"Honest, boys, I don't get this." Slim was clearly bewildered. "So he's a Catholic. So Catholics can't get divorced."

"Tell her, Jonesy," Joe said.

"You tell her," Jupiter said. "I've got business in a cemetery."

He left them and trotted out to his car, blowing on his fingers. The places a murder case takes a man!

19

Artistically, he thought driving rapidly back to the village, the theory must be right. Potter had to have hidden his gold in a cemetery; it was too simple not to be true. There had been Wren's idea of Logical Landmarks, Susan's unwitting remark to Betty about the names, and finally Arnold's excuse to Dexter for not appearing on Wednesday to finish digging his ditch—he'd had to cut the grass in the cemetery to prepare for a funeral. Malvina, Samantha, Amity... "old-fashioned names, like you see on gravestones." Logical Landmarks, indeed! Old Hiram had been literal enough—if you're going to bury something bury it in a burying ground! What a thrill Arnold must have had when it dawned on him!

He was excited and anxious to prove himself right but it was necessary to stop in the village. There were at least four cemeteries in town and he didn't know which one the Potter family had patronized. Vito would know, or Tom.

As it happened the Dexters were in the liquor store buying gin and they greeted him happily enough.

"How're things going?" Harry asked.

"Fine. Just fine."

"I think it's simply marvelous they made you Chief of Police," Dot said. "Has anything exciting been happening?"

"No. It's been pretty dull. Police work is mostly routine, you know. I'm the plodding type."

"How well I know that!" she said. "Then you haven't heard the really exciting news of the day?"

"What's that?"

"Really, Dot!" Harry protested. "We were asked not to tell."

"Oh, the poor darlings won't be able to keep it to themselves," she said. "Tom and Ginny are going to get married!"

"No!" said Jupiter.

"Thassa right, Boss!" said Vito, surprisingly. "She come in an' tella me all about it!"

"You see?" Dot said, smiling at Harry.

"We're having them over for a drink," Dexter explained. "Can you get Betty and join us?"

"Later maybe. Right now..." He paused, thinking it might be fun to make a small production out of the Potter treasure. After all, he'd had a fairly taxing day and it would do no harm to get a little credit for it all. "Where's Tom now?"

"They're just locking up the store."

Jupiter turned to Vito. "Have you solved that problem I gave you yet?"

Vito shook his head.

"Care to come along while I solve it for you?"

"Who'sa kiddin' who?"

Just then Tom and Ginny appeared at the door.

"What's the matter with the service in here?" Tom asked, winking at Vito. He had evidently been home for a shave and change of clothes.

"We're coming right along, Tom," Harry said.

"Wait a minute, I have a question," Jupiter said. "Who knows where Hiram Potter is buried?"

He had their attention and there was a moment of surprised silence.

"Do you mean Hiram himself?" Tom asked, frowning. And when Jupiter nodded, "Turkey Hill."

"Do they still use that cemetery?"

"Sure. Old Mrs. Swift was buried there Thursday."

"That's the place," said Jupiter happily. "It's also the place where Potter hid his money. Who'd like to go have a look?"

Everyone started talking at once but it appeared they'd very much like to go along for a look. Vito called to his wife to look after the store and they went outside. Dr. Wren was just coming out of the drugstore with his evening paper.

204

"Papers just came in," he said, holding it out. "Look, it's on the front page!"

There was a picture of Arnold's shack, and an inset of Howland, Jupiter had uncannily foretold the headline to McCoy. It read: CRAZED INDIAN SOUGHT IN SAXON SLAYING. He didn't bother to read the story. Ginny and Tom had already climbed into the back of the Dexters' jeep and Vito was in the front seat of Jupiter's car.

"We're on our way out to Turkey Hill, Doctor. I believe the treasure was hidden there."

Wren's reaction was not as violent as his earlier one but it was satisfactory enough. His mouth dropped open and the paper nearly slipped out of his fingers. "Not really!"

"Care to come along?"

"Turkey Hill? Do you mean the cemetery?"

"Yes, Potter's buried there. It's a Logical Location, isn't it?"

"Good God! Why . . . why, it never occurred to me!"

"Amity, Virtue, Samantha. Names on gravestones." Jupiter was beginning to enjoy himself.

Wren put his hand on Jupiter's arm. "Jones, are you sure about this?"

"I haven't been out to look yet. But I'm pretty certain. Aren't you?"

"Why I . . ." He closed his eyes and rubbed his jaw with his fist. "Of course! You must be right! But it's extraordinary! Really! How did you guess?"

"I had help from a seven-year-old. Will you come?"

The doctor would certainly come, following along in his own car. Mrs. Wren was at the church helping to prepare a bean supper and he was not due there for half an hour.

"It does seem odd to be having the supper," he explained, "but they had a meeting and decided as long as the food was all ready and everything..."

"Sure," said Jupiter. "Good for morale."

"Of course, Howland wasn't a member of the congregation."

Shaking his head a little, Wren hurried along to his car and Jupiter got in beside Vito.

"Cocktail parties, bean suppers," he muttered. "I don't think people are taking this business very seriously, Vito."

"Aah. Bad thing happen, people get together. How you thinka Turkey Hill, huh?"

Following Dexter's jeep Jupiter told him about it. Vito slapped his knee when he'd finished. "Sonofagun!"

"Smart Chiefa da Police, huh?"

"Okay, Boss. Okay, I quit. Lissen, s'pose you thinka him two weeks, month ago? You dig up, keep da money?"

Without turning his head from the road Jupiter knew Vito was grinning at him. "Certainly. I could use ninety thousand dollars as well as the next man."

"No kiddin', Boss? You keep it?"

"Why should I give it to the Potters? They had seventy years to look for it."

Vito began to laugh. "Liar! G'damn liar, you! You give it up. You got conscience!"

"Listen, you clown, I wouldn't predict how anyone would act if they came face to face with a pile of gold. A man's conscience operates pretty much in ratio to the chances there are of his being found out, whatever he does. I think I'd keep it."

"Like hell you would. I know you, Boss."

"Don't be so sure what you know. You were all wrong about Mrs. Madison, incidentally."

By the time he'd finished telling about Slim and the freezer they had arrived at Turkey Hill. The graveyard, a small one, bordered the road at the crest of the hill and they left their cars and climbed the low stone wall. Thanks to Arnold the grass was neatly cut and, at one end, fresh flowers were massed around the new grave of old Mrs. Swift. Not many modern granite stones were in evidence among the older slate markers, indicating that few local families still held plots here.

Jupiter had expected to find evidence of digging operations as soon as he entered the cemetery but, looking around, he saw no indication that the grass had been disturbed anywhere.

"Here's the Potter Plot," Tom called and everyone gathered at Hiram's grave. He was surrounded by half a dozen female Potters but none of them bore a key name.

"Let's fan out and see what we can find," Jupiter suggested.

Almost at once Dot Dexter cried, "Here's a Virtue! Virtue Mason. Born in 1780, died in 1805. She didn't live long, poor girl!"

Forcing himself to walk, Jupiter went over, but before he got there Ginny was calling, "Got Amity!" and a moment later Harry announced a Patience. Jupiter discovered his hands were shaking. Arnold had not cut too close to the stones and tall grass was growing around all of them.

"Hey!" He went down on his knees in front of the gravestone Dot had located. By looking closely he could trace an area of turf roughly two feet wide and five feet long that had been carefully removed and put back in place.

"Bingo!" said Dot. "I don't think I've ever been so excited! Look, Doctor!"

Wren bent over and examined the grass at Jupiter's shoulder. "That's it, Jones! Arnold found it!"

"And a neat job he did of it, too," Jupiter said. His hands were still shaking.

"What are you looking at?" Harry called from his stone.

"It's been dug up, darling!" Dot answered.

"Well, Patience hasn't," Dexter called back and Jupiter ran over to look.

"Amity has been dug," Ginny announced.

"So has Samantha," said Tom. "Samantha

Rice. 1761–1847. She had a long life, at any rate."

"You're right, Harry," Jupiter said, after looking at the grave. "This one hasn't been touched!"

"Well, what are we waiting for?" Harry demanded. "I've got a shovel in the jeep!"

"Sonofagun!" Vito said, summing up the situation. He slapped Jupiter on the back and hopped up and down. "Sonofagun!"

"There're a couple still missing, aren't there?" Jupiter asked. "What about Malvina? And what was the other one?"

"Abigail," Tom said.

These were quickly located and found to have been dug like the others. "All right, Harry, get your shovel," Jupiter said.

Harry had sobered a bit. "Do you really think we ought to?"

"Certainly. As Chief of Police I authorize it. Wholly in line with the investigation. We've got to make sure the gold is really here."

They were all gathered at the grave of Patience Frost, 1802–1854, when Dexter came back with the shovel. He handed it to Jupiter and, a little self-consciously, he began to dig. But his self-consciousness didn't last long. After all, he told himself, half an hour ago I was in an igloo and an hour before that I was sticking a needle into Mrs. Madison. This made some sense although it was a bit strenuous, coming after a full day.

"If he divided it evenly there should be fifteen thousand in here, shouldn't there?" Tom asked. "That's worth digging for."

"Who'd have suspected Arnold of such a nice sense of humor?" Dot asked. She was sitting on a nearby tombstone, smoking.

"How's that?" Jupiter asked.

"Patience. He left her to the last."

"So he did," said Dr. Wren and chuckled.

"Any time you get tired," Tom offered.

"I'm tired already," Jupiter said and gave him the shovel.

Harry, with his hands on his hips, was standing beside Wren. "I don't understand why, if he had found the gold, Arnold locked us in there last night."

"He didn't lock you in," Jupiter said. "Slim did."

He was getting a little tired of exclamations and explanations but he patiently went through it for them, concluding, "Maney told Howland Arnold was around there. That's why he went to the shack. I don't know what actually happened when he got there but I suppose Arnold might have been counting his gold and Howland caught him at it."

Dexter was having a great deal of difficulty accepting the fact that Slim had locked the door.

"She's just a playful little girl, darling," Dot said and Jupiter wondered how much she knew about Harry's infatuation. At the moment he didn't particularly care; he'd been involved enough today with the secret life of individual Saxons to hold him for some time. He hoped Dot and Harry would be able in some way to improve their married life but he was through offering suggestions to them. He also hoped Tom and Ginny would work things out but, after a private conversation someday with Ginny about Tom's mother, he'd leave them alone, too. As for Slim and Maney and Joe Bateman, well, they were adults and on their own. The life of a *deus ex machina* was too strenuous for him. It was giving him a headache.

The hole grew deeper. Harry spelled Tom and then Vito took over. Dr. Wren offered to take his turn but was refused, apparently on the grounds that he was too old for the work. The doctor had said nothing to the others about his own search for the treasure and Jupiter was willing to keep this secret as he had about Wren's drinking habits.

He thought about Arnold hiding in the swamp and McCoy and his men waiting for him to come out. This did not improve his headache. Poor Arnold! For thirty years he had looked for the gold and when he found it... But had he found it?

"What's the matter?" It was Ginny who had seen the shock come into his face.

"Nothing," he said quickly. "I was thinking about Arnold."

"I know," she said. "I don't like to think about him either. It's horrible."

His mind was racing now, going back over last night, the finding of Howland this morning, Arnold's excuse for not working at Dexter's. What if...? Yes, that could be it! It must be it!

"Yes," he said to Ginny. "Yes, it is horrible." He'd have to check it, of course. Right now it was simply a pattern, but a logical and damning pattern of violence. "Here, Vito, take a break."

He took the shovel and dug savagely to release the tension he was feeling. There was sand under the topsoil and the shovel slid in cleanly, taking large chunks like snow.

"My!" Dot said, watching him. "You look like a terrier."

He was waist deep in the trench, sweat running into his eyes, when he struck something solid. It felt like a stone but then, as he cleared around it, he saw the top of a small earthenware crock.

"That's it!" Tom yelled and they all crowded up to look.

Jupiter dropped the shovel, went to his knees, and worked the crock free, lifting it out of the trench. He took off the top and there were the coins, heaped bright and yellow inside. Painted neatly on the side of the crock was the figure, $17,500. It should have been a high moment but his only thought was, "What a hell of a damned way for a man to bank!"

Dot went to her knees, put both hands into the crock, scooped up a mound of coins, and let them fall back in a clinking stream through her fingers. "Love!" The expression on her face was sensual, almost wholly free of avarice.

It was necessary for them all to touch the gold, to pick up at least one of the twenty-dollar pieces, to weigh it, put it back, and take up another. He knew it was a natural reaction to the ancient magic, the ancient reality, of gold, and watching them, himself unmoved by it, he knew that his answer had to be right. At any other moment he too would have yielded to the spell of the gold but now he felt only disgust for it and the tragedy it had caused. He picked up the cover and quickly and somewhat shamefaced they dropped their coins back into the crock. He reached in himself and brought out a handful.

"Souvenirs. This can be classed as a directors' meeting."

He handed one each to Ginny, Tom, the Dexters, and Vito. Dr. Wren had moved a little way off. "Here, Doctor," Jupiter said and with his thumb flipped a coin so that it arched shining in the sun into his hand.

"Do you really think we . . ." Wren began.

"Certainly!" said Dot. "At that, I think we're showing remarkable restraint. Take several, Jupiter. One each for the children."

He smiled at her, put one in his pocket, and

replaced the lid. He climbed out of the trench and stretched. "So much for that."

"Nice going, Jupe," Tom said. "Congratulations."

"This certainly calls for a celebration," Harry said. "Will you get Betty and come over to the house?"

Jupiter thought quickly and then nodded. "All right. I'll see if we can get someone to stay with the children."

"Doctor? Will you join us?"

"I . . . I'm afraid I'm due at the church, Harry."

Dexter put his hand on Vito's shoulder. "How about you, Vito?"

"Aah!" said Vito, grinning and shaking his head. "I sella him. Never touch myself."

"Well, come on then," Harry said, picking up his shovel. "We'll give you a ride back to town anyway."

"Okay," said Vito and turned to Jupiter. "What you do witha crock, Boss?"

"I'll look after it. Don't worry. No more samples."

"Well, then we'll see you later," Dot said and they started for the jeep.

Tom held out his hand to Jupiter. "I really mean it, Jupe. That was good going."

"Thanks, Tom. I notice you've been home."

"Yes. Everything's set there, too. We're invited for supper, Ginny and I."

"Oh? Well, fine." He smiled at Ginny. "Have fun."

She smiled back, took Tom's arm, and they went along after the Dexters and Vito.

"It's really incredible, Jones," Wren said, remaining. "I can still hardly believe it!"

"Yes." And then, in a moment, when the jeep had started off, he looked straight at Wren and asked the question he'd been dreading, but the question he had to ask. "Tell me, Doctor, what did you do with Arnold's body?"

20

The sun was nearly down to the top of the tall pines at the back of the cemetery and the gravestones cast long shadows on the green grass. Wren remained motionless, his shadow stretching out and over the stone of Patience Frost, 1802–1854. His lips were pressed tight together and he looked back at Jupiter without blinking. And then he frowned. "I really don't know what you mean, Jones." There was courage in the attempt but his voice, breaking slightly, betrayed him. "Really, I don't know what you mean. Arnold's body?"

Jupiter felt a stirring of nausea and swallowed. "I wish to hell you didn't know what I mean. I'm sincere in that." He moved back and sat on the gravestone, his feet at the edge of the trench. "None of it was necessary, was it? If only we'd known Slim had locked the door last night instead of Arnold. But it certainly looked as if Arnold had done it, didn't it? You thought he'd tried to kill you and he certainly had a motive.

You killed him in self-defense almost, didn't you?"

"Really, Jones, I don't know what you're talking about!" He had more control over his voice now but he hadn't moved from the spot where he was standing.

Jupiter went on, talking softly, almost in a monotone. "You did a very neat job here, much neater than Arnold ever would have done. No one would have known about it if old Mrs. Swift hadn't died and Arnold hadn't been sent to cut the grass. That was on Wednesday. It was Wednesday night he was waiting for you here, wasn't it? When you made the deal? You had to trust each other, of course. There was no other way out of it. I imagine he was in a hurry to get it all dug up but you were against that. There was plenty of time and it took time to do the job right, to finish it up the way you did so that no one walking through here would know anything had been touched."

"You're making a serious charge. If you have any proof..."

"I haven't any proof, that's quite true. But why was Arnold at Maney's at all last night? If he'd found the treasure alone, why wasn't he here digging it up? You had to go to the party last night. Your wife probably insisted on it. Arnold was there checking up on you. There was only one crock to go and he wasn't taking any chances you'd dig that one up by yourself and leave town with the whole works. You have the other crocks, haven't you? You convinced Arnold it would be better for you to get rid of the gold and pay him off in cash, didn't you? Was he satisfied with that arrangement?"

"I have no gold, Jones. I certainly did not kill Arnold. I don't know what you're talking about at all." He rubbed one hand across his forehead. "If you weren't such a friend of mine I'd be tempted to have you up in court for what you've said already. I mean it! I...I'll sue you, Mr. Jones!"

"I wish, I honestly wish, you had a case, Doctor. I wouldn't mind being sued at all. But I'm not wrong about this. You killed Arnold and while you were there Howland happened to drive up because Maney had sent him. You saw the car drive in and thought very fast indeed. Arnold was dead and you took his shotgun and waited for Howland. When he stepped inside you killed him. It had to be that way."

Wren's face had been white, now slowly it began to go red. "You have no proof at all!" His voice was high.

"Suppose we look in your well, Doctor. The well you dump your empty bottles into. Is Arnold's body in there?"

It had been a shot in the dark but not too wild a one at that. Wren's abandoned well was a logical location.

"Shall we go and have a look?" he repeated.

And then Wren finally moved. His hand went into his pocket and while Jupiter watched, unable to move himself, it came out with a small, nickel-plated revolver.

"I'm sorry, very sorry. I'm going to have to kill you, Jones."

Jupiter didn't move from the gravestone. He was terrified but beyond that he should have guessed Wren would have a gun! Even Maney had had a gun! What a fool...But this wasn't a drunken jealous Maney, this was a cornered killer fighting for his life!

"Don't be foolish," Jupiter said evenly. "I haven't any intention of turning you in. I never had."

The gun didn't waver. "I'm going to kill you."

"Put it away, Doctor," he said and forced himself to smile. "We're going to do business. I'm no policeman. You've got what, about seventy-five thousand dollars, no one knows about except me? I'll split with you. What do you think I am, a damned fool? Neither of us can bring Howland and Arnold back to life. It was simply an accident they were killed anyway." If he doesn't shoot in the next thirty seconds... "I'm not even taking a chance. The police believe Arnold killed Howland, that he's got the treasure and hidden it himself. What chance are we taking? You were ready to split with Arnold. Now you can split with me."

"I couldn't trust you." It was a statement of fact but in it there was hope, a temptation to take a way out.

"Kill me and you're finished. You have to

trust me. Are you afraid of my conscience? I'm
no Harry Dexter, Wren. I'm honest when it
pays to be, like everyone else. Don't you think I
understand how you felt when you found this
gold? Before you found it you were ready to
give it to the Potters and keep your 25 per cent.
But then when you actually had it in your
hands you changed your mind. Do you think I
can't use thirty-five thousand dollars? I have an
income of four thousand a year and three children to raise." He spat between his teeth into
the trench at his feet. He had shaved his actual
income as low as he dared.

"If I didn't have this gun you'd have arrested
me. I'm certain of that. Don't deny it." Wren
was fighting his desire to be convinced.

"I do deny it. Strongly. What kind of a fool
do you think I am? Do you think I give a God
damn if society punishes you or not? Your puny
little crime is meaningless to me and to the
world. There's a murder every forty-five minutes in this country alone and 60 per cent of
them are never solved. In this age it's every
man for himself and no holds barred. Put that
gun away and let's talk business!" He started to
stand up.

"*No!*" The gun was trembling now in Wren's
hand. "I can't trust you!"

Jupiter sat back, sighed, and spread his
hands. "All right. I give up. Shoot me. Add one
more senseless murder to your list. What will
you do when you meet my wife and children?

Will you like that? Arnold and Howland are one thing, aren't they? Maybe in time you could get them off your conscience. Will you enjoy your gold when you think of my wife and children, Doctor?"

It was the wrong approach. Wren was nearly at the breaking point and any appeal to his conscience was useless. Jupiter had to offer him a way out.

"All right," he said quickly. "There's another thing you can do. We'll fix it so both murders can be pinned on me. Then you'll be sure you can trust me."

"I . . . I don't understand."

"Simple. Keep me covered while I drive to your house. We get Arnold out of the well and put him in the trunk of my car. Later tonight we'll bury him on my property. Do you think I'd dare go to the police tomorrow and tell them I'd found him in your well? Think how it would look! I found the gold here just now. No one knows you were even looking for it. I'd be convicted in nothing flat. I'd have to trust you."

There were so many loopholes in this that Jupiter was sure Wren would see them at once. But he hesitated, thinking about it. The temptation to get Arnold out of his own well at any cost must have been tremendous. Wren was turned with his back to the road and Jupiter, out of the corner of his eye, saw Maney's truck pull up behind his own car at the other end of the cemetery.

"It's your only choice, Doctor," he said quickly, not looking again toward the road. "I'm willing to frame myself because I'm certain the police will never learn the truth. I want that money. You want that money. Let's be realistic. Let's take the right way out." It was an actual physical effort to keep from looking toward the road now.

"No. You think too fast. You're too clever. I can't trust you." He said it almost sadly and his arm came up, pointing the gun at Jupiter's head. And then there was a rifle shot from the road and the pistol was knocked out of his hand.

Jupiter lunged forward from the tombstone and put his foot on Wren's gun. Dazed, the doctor, not holding his bleeding wrist, turned around.

A rather touching tableau took place on the road. Standing beside the truck Slim slowly lowered the rifle and then Joe came around to her side and she put her head against his chest. His arms went around her.

21

"Yes, a rather full day. An emotional day," Jupiter said, much later.

The highly unpleasant business of handing Wren over to McCoy, of hearing his full confession, of removing Arnold's body from the well, had been done. To others had been allocated the still more unpleasant job of seeking out Mrs. Wren at the bean supper and breaking the news to her. Tomorrow he would call on her, perhaps, and offer his condolences but seeing her tonight he deserved to be spared. All six crocks of gold were now reposing in the safe at the town hall where, with little formality, Jupiter had resigned as Chief of Police.

"Yes. A kind of day one hopes to avoid by moving to the country."

It was growing dark and they were sitting on their porch, about to be driven in by the mosquitoes. Betty, holding his hand, said, "I don't think you told me where Wren hid the crocks he'd already dug up."

"In his compost heap. A symbolic choice, I feel. I have some sympathy for him and then again I have sympathy for the victims. He strangled Arnold, drunkenly asleep on his miserable cot. There's a nightmarish scene for you. An oil lamp burning, the cheap nude pictures on the wall, Howland coming in to discover him..."

"Don't! Were you really sure Wren had done it when you confronted him in the cemetery?"

"It had to be that way. If Arnold had killed Howland he wouldn't have run off and left everything like that. And then there was old Ginger. The dog did pick up some kind of a trail there, near the shack. That was probably where Wren dragged Arnold's body down to his car. The whole enterprise at the cemetery pointed to Wren having found the gold, of course. Even leaving Patience's grave until the last pointed to him. Arnold wouldn't have bothered with humor as subtle as that."

They were silent for a time. A mosquito bit Jupiter's ankle and he slapped at it.

"There's just one question that bothers me a little," she said.

"Yes?"

"Suppose Wren had agreed to share the money with you. Would you have turned him over to McCoy anyway?"

"Don't be childish," he answered shortly. "Of course I would. He was threatening to kill me.

There was no moral question involved." He thought a minute. "Or is there?"

"That's what I wondered."

"Well, I was justified in trying to save my life, but to welsh on him later... I don't know. I'm glad the choice didn't come up. It's a tough one." He stood up and walked to the end of the porch and back. "If I hadn't turned him in and McCoy had found out about it somehow, later on, I'd have gone to jail. You realize that, don't you?"

"Oh, sure. Honestly, I don't want you to worry about it, darling. I don't know why I brought it up."

He sat down again beside her. "I'll tell you the answer. Either I'd have turned him in or I wouldn't have. Once I'd made up my mind it wouldn't bother me. We're always being faced with questions of personal integrity and we always will be. Only saints are infallible."

"That's ducking it nicely, dear." She patted his hand. "I spent a very uneasy day and I suppose it's only fair you should spend an uneasy night."

He suspected he was in for a series of uneasy nights. It was all very well to tell himself he didn't care what happened from now on to the Dexters, Mrs. Madison, Tom and Ginny, Maney, and Slim and Joe, but the fact remained that his actions had, however minutely, influenced their lives. Certainly he had influenced the life of the Wrens!

He had come out of his cautious social isolation with a bang. And it had affected him like strong drink on an empty stomach; he had surely been on a short binge of commitment this day! But was he due for a hangover? Individual acts were not subject to the same kind of criticism as a work of art. Once again, as he had done last night, he had better forgive himself and not try to add up a balance. There was a certain wild logic in Arnold's method of bookkeeping. You simply examined and put down the wisdom or the folly, the good or the evil, of your impulsive actions, but you never added them up. If you were ahead of the game, you slept. That should be enough for anyone.

A car turned into the driveway and he saw it was Maney's truck. Joe was driving.

"Hi," Slim called from the cab. "We brought you the television, Jonesy!"

He had an impulse to thank her but to say he didn't want it. He was really very tired and his head was aching worse than ever.

"Fine!" he said. "Bring her in!"

The machine was carried into the kitchen and drinks were made and distributed. Betty raised her glass to Slim, "To your marksmanship!"

"Gee, thanks, dear. It was nothin'."

"Merely his life," Betty said and took Jupiter's arm. She had never been far from his side from the time he'd got home.

Joe said, "I keep thinking about it, Jonesy.

226

Suppose we hadn't met Dexter in town and decided to go and have a look at the cemetery?"

"Don't think about it," Jupiter said. "A few things have to work out right in this life. Let's not question how they happen."

"What a caper!"

Suddenly Jupiter realized this was exactly what Slim and Joe felt about the thing. It was just another absorbing incident in their young, tough lives. Whatever happened to them, at least, they could handle. All at once and for the first time he felt solidly middle-aged.

"By the way," he asked, rolling the cold glass across his forehead, "who won that ball game?"

"Didn't you hear?" Betty asked. "Williams got another in the twelfth!"

"Good for old Ted!"

There would always be baseball.

27 million Americans can't read a bedtime story to a child.

It's because 27 million adults in this country simply can't read.

Functional illiteracy has reached one out of five Americans. It robs them of even the simplest of human pleasures, like reading a fairy tale to a child.

You can change all this by joining the fight against illiteracy.

Call the Coalition for Literacy at toll-free **1-800-228-8813** and volunteer.

**Volunteer
Against Illiteracy.
The only degree you need
is a degree of caring.**

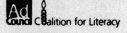

Ad Council Coalition for Literacy